"My head tells ... fall in love agai...

"But my crazy heart has decided it likes you," Burke said, taking her hand in his.

She felt his fingers close more firmly over hers. "Mine, too." She met his stormy-looking eyes. "But I'm scared, Burke. Scared as hell. You're going to be gone in a month. You're never comin' back."

"I know...." Burke clearly read the frustration in her face, felt it in his own heart.

"I'm just not built emotionally for an affair, Burke."

"I know that. That's why I've been fighting my attraction to you. But it isn't easy, Angel. It isn't easy at all...."

Dear Reader,

Love is in the air, but the days will certainly be sweeter if you snuggle up with this month's Special Edition offerings—and a box of decadent chocolates. First up, award-winning author and this year's President of Romance Writers of America®, Shirley Hailstock is a fresh new voice for Special Edition, but fans already know what a gifted storyteller she is. With numerous novels and novellas under her belt, Shirley debuts in Special Edition with *A Father's Fortune*, which tells the story of a day-care-center owner and her foster child who teach a grumpy carpenter how to face his past and open his heart to love.

Lindsay McKenna packs a punch in *Her Healing Touch,* a fast-paced read from beginning to end. The next in her widely acclaimed MORGAN'S MERCENARIES: DESTINY'S WOMEN series, this romance details the trials of a beautiful paramedic who teaches a handsome Special Forces officer the ways of her legendary healing. *USA TODAY* bestselling author Susan Mallery *completely* wins us over in *Completely Smitten*, next up in her beloved series HOMETOWN HEARTBREAKERS. Here, an adventurous preacher's daughter seeks out a new life, but never expects to find a new *love* with a sexy U.S. marshal.

The fourth installment in Crystal Green's KANE'S CROSSING miniseries, *There Goes the Bride* oozes excitement when a runaway bride is spirited out of town by a reclusive pilot she once loved in high school. Patricia McLinn delights her readers with *Wedding of the Century*. Here, a heroine returns to her hometown seven years after running out of her wedding. When she faces her jilted groom, she realizes their feelings are stronger than ever! Finally, in Leigh Greenwood's *Family Merger*, sparks fly when a workaholic businessman meets a good-hearted social worker, who teaches him the meaning of love.

Don't miss this array of novels that deliver an emotional charge and satisfying finish you're sure to savor, no matter what the season!

Happy Valentine's Day!

Karen Taylor Richman
Senior Editor

Please address questions and book requests to:
Silhouette Reader Service
U.S.: 3010 Walden Ave., P.O. Box 1325, Buffalo, NY 14269
Canadian: P.O. Box 609, Fort Erie, Ont. L2A 5X3

Lindsay McKenna

HER HEALING TOUCH

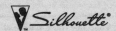

SPECIAL EDITION™

Published by Silhouette Books

America's Publisher of Contemporary Romance

To my husband, David,
whose love has always been healing for me.

SILHOUETTE BOOKS

ISBN 0-373-24519-X

HER HEALING TOUCH

Books by Lindsay McKenna

LINDSAY McKENNA

teaches at the Desert Institute of Classical Homeopathy in Phoenix, Arizona. When she isn't teaching, she is writing books about love. She feels love is the single greatest healer in the world.

Dear Reader,

The heroines of DESTINY'S WOMEN, all members of the Black Jaguar Squadron, are a bestselling hit—thanks to all of you! I'm thrilled my readers like these confident women who fight in the drug war in South America and around the world. I can't tell you how many letters and e-mails I've received from you asking for more of this series. Well, here's a brand-new story, featuring Sergeant Angel Paredes, a Peruvian Army woman and paramedic who flies with the supersecret United States black ops, the Black Jaguar Squadron. Angel is legendary for her healing powers and has been known to pull people back from the brink of death! Now, you will find out why she has this talent and how it leads her to the love of a lifetime.

This March, look for the next member of the Black Jaguar Squadron, when DESTINY'S WOMEN continues with Chief Warrant Officer Cam Anderson's story, *An Honorable Woman*, available from Silhouette Books. If you want to read more about these extraordinary women, please write to Silhouette and let them know!

Warmly,

Lindsay McKenna

Chapter One

"**D**ude, this sucks," Sergeant Angel Paredes muttered as she sat sulking on the gurney in the Black Jaguar Squadron dispensary.

Dr. Elizabeth Cornell studied the X rays she had put up on the light box. "Hmm. Well, Angel, you did it up right this time." Tracing the X ray of Angel's left shoulder with an index finger, Elizabeth turned to look at her assistant. "Your biceps tendon is inflamed. You have tendonitis. Congratulations."

"Damn…"

"Yeah, no kidding," Elizabeth said, quirking her lips. "You know what that means?"

"That you're gonna give me an anti-inflammatory shot to ease my considerable pain, so I stop acting like an irritable pit bull. Right?"

Grinning, Elizabeth turned off the light box and put the two X rays into a large folder that had Angel's name at the top. The dispensary shook and trembled as two Apache helicopter gunships began powering up for takeoff. The whole Black Jaguar operation was hidden in a cave complex within a mountain fifty miles from the archeological wonder Machu Picchu, and the picturesque tourist town of Agua Caliente. The alarm had rung earlier, which meant the two pilot crews on duty would be intercepting a drug shipment flight somewhere near Peru's border with Bolivia.

"I'm going to save the squadron from my bad mood," Angel said once the trembling had subsided. "I'll bet I get written up for a commendation on it."

"Very funny, Angel," Elizabeth said, rummaging in another cabinet. "Even the Angel of Death looks like death warmed over," she continued, casting a grin at her faithful assistant, a paramedic with the Peruvian army. Angel held her left arm guardedly against her body, her right hand cradling it.

"Sorry, bad pun. I couldn't help myself," Elizabeth murmured sympathetically as she filled a syringe with the pain-relieving drug she knew Angel needed.

"I'm no crybaby, Doc, not even at a time like this. I'm one hundred percent Incan Indian," she muttered defiantly. Her ancestors were known for their ability to handle pain.

Though she tried to rise to the occasion, Angel didn't have her usual spunk and feistiness, Elizabeth realized as she flicked her finger against the syringe and approached her colleague. "Hey, you're in a lotta pain. It shows."

Angel eyed Elizabeth, the only physician on staff at BJS. They'd been teamed up together nearly three and a half years and worked like a well-oiled machine. "Dude, I never knew an inflamed tendon could make me throw up and then pass out."

"Hmm, well, pain can do those things to you. You just lifted one heavy box of supplies too many from that Blackhawk helicopter, and did your tendon in." She moved to Angel's bared left shoulder. Elizabeth had had to cut away the patient's T-shirt to examine her injury earlier, when one of the crew had brought Angel in on a gurney, passed out.

"This is so humiliating...." Angel watched as Elizabeth lifted the needle in her direction. "What are you gonna do? Put the needle right into that inflamed tendon? Am I gonna pass out from pain again?''

Cupping her shoulder gently, Elizabeth murmured, ''Relax. I'm the best shot-giver on the face of the earth. This won't hurt, I promise....''

Angel sucked in a breath and shut her eyes tightly. She barely felt the prick of the needle. And just as Elizabeth had promised, there was no pain.

''There,'' her friend murmured, pleased with her efforts as she gently swabbed the area with a cotton ball drenched in alcohol. ''All over.''

''And relief from this gutting pain is right around the corner, right, Doc?'' Angel asked weakly.

''Yep.'' Dropping the syringe into the designated wastebasket, Elizabeth pulled off her latex gloves and dropped them in there as well.

''What does this mean? How long am I gonna be laid up and useless?''

''Well, you've really injured that tendon, but by resting your shoulder and not lifting heavy items and limiting your mobility, I think in four to six weeks you'll be back in the saddle again.''

Eyes widening, Angel gasped. ''What? Four weeks?''

''I said four to six weeks.'' Elizabeth turned to her and studied her dark brown eyes, which were filled with worry. She handed Angel another dark green T-shirt and helped her get it on. "Four would be minimum. And even if it is completely healed in that time, you're looking at occupational therapy exercises to regain and support the muscles around that tendon. You also—" she patted Angel's other shoulder gently "—need to learn your weight-lifting limits. And how to lift in order to never have this happen again. Next time—" she held Angel's mutinous stare "—it may mean surgery or partial loss of mobility in your arm. Now, that's enough of a death sentence that it should make even you— the Peruvian superwoman—think about the consequences. And I know that look, Angel. I know what you're thinking. You're thinking you're going to heal up in a jiffy and be back at work in a week. It isn't gonna happen, so get over it and roll with this one—the right way."

"B-but…what about you? I'm the only paramedic at BJS. You *need* me, Doc. You can't get along without me. What are you gonna do? You can't handle this place by yourself, and I can't be a one-armed paramedic. What if one of our Apaches gets fired on by a Kamov Black Shark drug helo, and pilots get wounded? You're gonna need my help."

"I know…."

Opening her good hand, desperation in her tone, Angel added, "You gotta get a stand-in—a temporary paramedic—up here."

"I know."

Morosely, Angel looked around the quiet dispensary. The aluminum Quonset hut sat at the very back of the huge lava cave that housed the entire black ops base. "Dude, this sucks."

"You said it, Angel." Elizabeth gave her a slight smile. "Listen, I'm authorizing you four weeks of sick leave. I want you to go back to the barracks and rest. Put a hot pack on that shoulder from time to time and alternate it with an ice pack. Rest, sleep, drink plenty of water, and leave that shoulder alone. Don't pick up anything with that arm, you hear?"

Glumly, Angel looked around. Already the pain was beginning to ease, and she was grateful. "Yeah…I hear you, Doc. No sling, right?"

"No, not at this time. Just be careful how you move it around, is all. But if you reinjure it, Angel, I'll have to put one on you."

"That's good news." Angel brightened. "At least I'll save what's left of my Inca pride."

Elizabeth grinned. "Get outta here."

Carefully sliding off the gurney, Angel continued cradling her bad arm against her body; it was the only position that felt comfortable right now. Pushing open the dispensary door with the toe of her black GI boot, she headed down the hall, then left the metal structure. Looking up, she saw bright shafts of sunlight flickering through the Eye, a large hole in the lava wall that protected the huge landing area and the rest of the cave. It was 1000. The day was young. And she was screwed. Glaring toward the Blackhawk helicopter, where she'd injured herself unloading supplies, she saw that all the boxes were stacked on a pallet on an electric golf cart, ready for distribution. Who was going to unpack all the medical supplies that would be dropped off? The doctor was up to her hocks in work. And Angel was useless to her now with only one good hand available.

Frowning, she ruffled her short black hair, then pulled her soft green army cap from the back pocket of the jungle-green-and-brown camouflage pants she wore. Settling the cover on her head and positioning the bill so it protected her eyes from the sudden bright light cascading into the cave, she headed for the headquarters building, which sat off to one side. She was going to talk to their commanding officer, Major Maya Stevenson.

The knock on her open door made Maya lift her head from the relentless paperwork that encircled her like a wagon train on her green, army-issue metal desk.

"Enter," she called, wondering who it was. When she saw the Angel of Death, Maya frowned. Angel had earned that name from her legendary ability to cheat death by rescuing people from the door of it.

"Ma'am? May I have a moment of your time? I know you're busy," Angel said in a rush as she came to attention in front of the major's desk. She saluted carefully, keeping her left side immobile.

Maya returned the salute. "At ease, Sergeant."

"Thank you, ma'am," Angel replied, automatically cradling her left arm.

"I heard what happened."

"Already?"

Lips twitching, Maya sat back. "You know how word gets around here, Angel. Telepathically."

Laughing a little, though it hurt to do even that, Angel nodded. "I guess one of the crew told you?"

"Yeah." Maya rose and came around the desk. She pulled one of the green metal chairs from a corner and brought it over. "Sit down, Angel. You look like death warmed over."

Touched by her C.O.'s care, Angel sat down. "You're the second person to use those exact words. Thank you, ma'am."

Maya grinned wryly. "How's the pain level?" she asked as she sauntered back to her desk and sat down.

Angel gestured awkwardly to her injured shoulder. "It's getting better by the moment. Doc gave me a shot of an anti-inflammatory into the tendon."

"Good. I once ruptured a tendon here—" Maya pointed to her left shoulder "—when I was a young girl. I was out climbing a tree, thinking I was Tarzan. Only my arms weren't very long and the branch I was swinging to was too much of a stretch...."

"Ouch. So you know what this feels like?"

Wryly, Maya said, "Yeah, I do."

Angel smiled. She always felt better when she was around Maya. The major was a woman steeped in mystery and mysticism. She was the reason the Black Jaguar Squadron even existed. Her black, shoulder-length hair shone beneath the fluorescent lights, curling slightly on her proud shoulders. Like all her pilots, Maya wore a black flight uniform that had no insignias, except for one—the Black Jaguar Squadron patch, sewn on the left upper arm.

Reaching toward one of the piles of paperwork, Maya said, "I think we might have an answer for this predicament, however. A real godsend."

"Oh?"

"You're here because you're worried the doc will need help you can't provide, right?"

Angel never got used to her C.O.'s uncanny ability to seemingly read her mind. As a Quero Indian, steeped in the traditions of her Incan ancestors, Angel understood how energy could be used in many inexplicable ways. Telepathy, as far as she was concerned, was energy sent from one person's brain to another, much like a telephone call without the cord between them. She had come to expect it from Maya.

"Er…yes, ma'am…."

With a brief smile, Maya dangled a file in front of her.

"I think our collective prayers have been answered in a highly synchronistic development. Take a look at this file for a moment while I fill you in." Maya handed it across the desk. "I just got this request last week, as a matter of fact." Leaning back in her creaky chair, she laced her long fingers across her belly. "As you know by now, our little black ops down here, which was the laughingstock of the army when it began, has now become the darling of it. Amazing what time, diligence of effort and a fifty percent reduction of drug flights out of Peru will do to make the military look kindly upon us."

Angel nodded. "Yes, ma'am, we were just a renegade bunch of women when you created this operation, making that vision of yours a reality." Curious, she settled the file on her lap and opened it. There was a letter on the front page, a request.

"Well," Maya murmured humorously, "the U.S. Army is begging us to allow more of their men to come down here and train with us, in many capacities. They want their best pilots to learn from ours. Our flight crews refuel and rearm Apaches faster and better than anyone they've got up there in the U.S.A. I have crew specialists wanting to work with us and see how we do what we do. And—" she smiled at Angel "—now even Special Forces are sticking their nose into our black ops."

"Oh?"

"Yeah, that letter, which I want you to read, is from the head of Special Forces, General Rutherford. He wants a Sergeant Burke Gifford, an A team paramedic teacher, to come down here and train with *you*."

Angel's mouth dropped open in surprise. "Me?"

"Yes. Read on." Maya waved her hand at the file resting on Angel's lap.

Angel rapidly scanned the official-looking letter, which had been penned by the general. It was basically asking that Gifford be allowed to work with the paramedic at BJS in order to understand unique aspects and uses of their medical model, and how it might be utilized in other places of combat, black ops or not. Brows bunching, Angel read the last paragraph. "This is too much...." she murmured.

Maya chuckled. "Yeah, ain't it?"

Looking up, Angel said, "This general knows of me. He actually refers to me as the Angel of Death."

"Your legend precedes you, Paredes."

Maya's dry wit wasn't lost on her. Angel saw the spark of humor in her C.O.'s eyes.

"What I find interesting is that some of the little extracurricular activities you engage in, the tricks you employ as a Quero Indian, trained in your Incan traditions, is getting their attention."

Angel gulped. She'd always sensed that Maya knew about her mystical background, but it wasn't ever discussed, at least not openly as they were doing now. Rather, Maya simply accepted it as a part of her, just as Maya had her own mystical traditions.

"Er...ma'am..."

"You're in a pickle, Paredes." Maya chuckled indulgently, watching the twenty-eight-year-old paramedic sit there and blush. Angel had copper-colored skin, thick, short black hair and very large, wise-looking dark brown eyes. Like most Quero people, she was short and stocky and strong. Few knew the inner workings of the Quero, the royal bloodline of the Incas of the past. But Maya did. Knew them well.

"Your skill has gained the attention of a general. Now," Maya drawled, "if it was the sergeant putting in this request, I could blow him off and circular file it. As it is, your reputation for saving lives when the person shoulda croaked has reached General Rutherford's ears."

Gulping again, Angel said, "And you can't blow off a general. Right?"

"Bang on, Paredes. You're reading this one correctly."

"But," Angel sputtered, tapping the letter repeatedly with her index finger, "I *can't* teach them what I know! First of all, this guy—"

"Sergeant Gifford?"

"Yeah…him. Well, he wouldn't believe it, anyway. He's a paramedic. Undoubtedly dyed-in-the-wool and tied to the traditional Western medicine model."

Shrugging eloquently, Maya said, "The dude has some pull if he can get a general to write this proposal and request for him. He's the head medical instructor for all of Special Forces training. So he's got something going for him.''

Angel snorted softly. ''Yeah, it's called the curiosity of a cat, ma'am. That's all.''

''There's a photo of him on the next page. Take a look.''

Unsettled, Angel scowled and lifted the letter, finding a colored photo beneath. The man's face was square, his jaw hard and set. His gray eyes reminded Angel of a cat's, and for some reason that bothered her or perhaps drew her. She instantly rejected the latter possibility. Gifford was dressed in his Class A dark green army uniform, the red beret worn by Special Forces members in place on his dark brown hair. She saw the weathered lines at the corners of his eyes, indicating he spent a lot of time out-of-doors. His mouth was thinned and unsmiling. Of course, this was an official army photo, in which no one smiled. Still, she dug into the man's face, studying his craggy features, with her intuition open.

Gifford was not a pretty boy. She saw a scar above the dark, thick slash of his right eyebrow. His nose, strong and dominating, reminded her of a condor's beak. It had obviously been broken in the past. The merciless look in his light gray eyes, those black pupils huge and staring back at her, undid her for a moment.

"This dude don't take no prisoners, does he?"

Chuckling, Maya said, "Doesn't look like it on the surface."

"He's got a face like the Andes."

"Yeah, all lava and granite. Tough."

"I don't see compassion in him," Angel said, feeling energy drain from her. "I'm looking for something face-saving in this guy. I don't see it."

"I think he hides behind that mask in the photo," Maya said gently. "Don't panic on me, Paredes. It would be the first time I've seen you hit that button."

Lifting her head, Angel tried to smile. "Sorry, ma'am. I *am* rattled."

"Look at it this way," Maya counseled with a twisted smile. "You need help right now because of your injury. Gifford asked for six weeks, to tail you around to see what you do and how you do it as a paramedic for BJS. Let him be your hands while you train him in to help the doctor. He can be like a puppy following at your heels."

"What about my, er…other skills, ma'am? I don't have to show him that, do I?"

"No. Not unless you think it's right. We'd at least have a pair of hands here to help us while you recover. He's a trained paramedic. He can stand in for you, Angel, and help Elizabeth. Overall, it's a good fit for our present predicament.''

Mouth thinning, Angel took another look at Gifford's stiff, almost defiant expression. The man was like a hungry raptor ready to leap out of the photograph and grab her. Strangely, she felt her heart respond. She was confused. Gifford's face was not forgiving in any way. He was a professional soldier and there was absolutely no softness in him.

''He doesn't look like he's got a drop of sensitivity in him,'' she moaned. ''The women aren't gonna like that. We get along better with more responsive types.''

''Well,'' Maya said, ''if Gifford tries to strong-arm anyone here, I think they'll straighten him out pronto, don't you?''

Angel saw her C.O. grinning like a jaguar, her eyes narrowed slightly. ''That's true, we don't take guff from anyone—especially men.''

''Bang on, Paredes. You're the one who's gonna be saddled with him, and so you're the one whose gonna take it on the chin, so to speak. You're tough, though, and my bet's on you to stop this guy in his tracks should he decide that just because you're a woman—and petite—he can ignore you or run over you.''

Snorting, Angel growled, "He'd better not try."

"Yeah." Maya chortled softly. "Or he'll be asking for a transfer sooner rather than later. Try to be a bit kind to him? We need him around for at least four to six weeks, until you climb back into the saddle, okay?"

Feeling a little better, Angel closed the folder, stood up and handed it back. "Yes, ma'am, I'll do my best."

"Go tell the doctor what's comin' down, will you? And tell her if she has any other questions, to come see me."

"I will. I think she'll be relieved."

"I'm sure I'll hear a whoop and holler from that direction. Gifford's good at what he does, so he'll be able to fill your shoes, medically speaking, up to a point." Maya flashed her glittering, pantherlike smile. "But he's not the Angel of Death. That's why I need you to shepherd him around, use his skills, while you get yourself back on your feet ASAP. Okay?"

Heartened by her C.O.'s belief in her, Angel came to attention. "Yes, ma'am. Music to my ears."

"Get out of here, Paredes. Go get some rest and take care of that shoulder like the doc ordered."

Angel nodded. "Yes, ma'am. I will, now that

we've got some help coming our way. I was just worried for the doctor. She's really busy.''

''I know.''

Of course she would know, Angel thought as she saluted.

''Dismissed, Sergeant. Thanks for dropping by. And try to be kind to Gifford the first couple of days. I'm sure he's not used to a nearly all-women squadron.''

Chapter Two

Where in the hell am I being sent? It was a question Sergeant Burke Gifford asked himself many times as the Bell helicopter moved toward the narrow hole in the lava wall that would allow them entrance to the Black Jaguar Base in the jungle mountains of Peru. He was the only passenger, and had been picked up at the Cuzco airport along with a hefty load of supplies, which were anchored all around him by nylon netting.

It was early morning, the mists thick and swirling as the chopper hovered, slowly approaching the gaping hole in the black lava wall. Looking between the two front seats, occupied by women pilots, Burke glimpsed the "Eye," as they called it, for the first time.

Automatically, he tensed, reaching for the nylon netting around him and gripping it hard. The hole looked too small for the Bell helo to pass through. Yet as Burke sucked in a sudden breath and held it, the pilot maneuvered through it deftly as if it was nothing. Burke stared at the black rock wall as the helo moved through, noting how it glistened wetly from the mist—that's how close they'd come to it.

It was only when the chopper began to land on a rough slab of black lava inside the cave that Burke let out that breath of air. He had on a set of headphones, so he was privy to the chatter between the pilots and the ground crew. From their conversations, he could tell they weren't at all concerned about flying through that hole like he was. Marveling at the size of the cave, he felt his eyes widen even more as he looked around and grasped the enormity of this operation. What an incredible place! His respect for the base, and the people who ran it, mushroomed.

"Okay, Sergeant Gifford, you can breathe now," the pilot said with a chuckle.

Gifford managed a sick smile. "Thanks, Chief

Mabrey,'' he said to the woman they called ''Snake,'' as she twisted around to look at him with a huge grin.

''Our pleasure, Sergeant. I warned you that the Eye would get your attention.''

''It did, ma'am. My undivided attention.''

Chortling with delight, Snake unharnessed herself as the Bell helo powered down. The blades were turning more slowly now. No one could leave the helo until they stopped spinning.

''You'll get used to it after a while,'' the copilot said.

Gifford saw the other woman remove her helmet and fluff up her blond hair, which had a red streak running through it. Snake called her ''Wild Woman.'' That fit. Again he wondered what kind of crazy world he was entering. This was an essentially all-female black ops. He knew there were a few men assigned, but not many. For once, he was in the minority. Not something he'd encountered in his well-ordered world at the U.S. base where he taught. This was a complete turnaround.

''Ah,'' Wild Woman said, pointing through the cockpit window, ''there's the Angel of Death, Sergeant. She's waiting for you. See her? Over there? She's the one with her arm in a sling, looking very unhappy. Can't miss her.''

Unhooking his seat belt, Burke moved forward, bracing his hands on the metal walls behind the pilots' seats. Eyes narrowing, he studied the bustling activity on the lip of the cave below. Though the lighting was poor, he noted a woman in camouflage fatigues and black boots, her arm in a dark green sling, standing to one side with a frown on her coppery face.

"Yes, ma'am, I think I see her."

Wild Woman smiled, taking her knee board off her thigh and tucking it into the oversize pocket on the right leg of her uniform. "Sergeant Angel Paredes. She's saved more lives than we can count. You're lucky to be working with her for the next six weeks, Sergeant. She's an incredible person. She's got that sour look on her face because of her shoulder injury, which she got by lifting too heavy a box. Angel doesn't like being sick." Wild Woman laughed. "She's a lousy patient, believe me."

"That's what I heard," he murmured, trying to see her more clearly.

"She's a legend in her own time," Snake agreed, pulling off her own helmet.

"That's why I'm down here—to learn from her."

Snake grinned at Wild Woman. "Well, Angel is

a pistol, Sergeant. She shoots straight from the hip and takes no prisoners. Treat her right or you'll find yourself on her bad side.''

''Not a good thing,'' Wild Woman said seriously. ''A pit bull without a muzzle or leash.''

''Thanks for the warning.'' Burke saw that, under Angel Paredes's army cap, her short black hair framed her oval face. He knew from her personnel jacket that she was a Peruvian Indian, and her high cheekbones testified to the fact. She was short and compactly built, although even the bulky fatigues she wore could not hide her womanly assets. He could see she was curved in all the right places.

''Nope, you don't mess with the Angel of Death,'' Snake murmured good-naturedly as she sized up the Special Forces sergeant. ''Respect her and you'll live another day.''

The blades stopped turning. Immediately, a crew hooked up the nosewheel of the helo to a transport vehicle and pulled the craft deep within the cave. Once the helo was taken to the revetment area, the blades were tethered and tied down. Burke heard the door on the cargo bay slide open. One of the crew women looked inside.

''Welcome to BJS, Sergeant. Want to come with me?''

''Sure.'' Thanking the pilots who'd transported

him, Burke turned and made his way through the stacks of supplies to the door. When he'd leaped lightly to the cave floor, the crew woman pointed toward Angel. ''That's her, Sergeant—your sponsor. Take off and we'll see that your duffel bag is brought to your quarters.''

''Thanks.'' Burke nodded and headed where she'd pointed. Focusing on Sergeant Paredes, he felt his heart suddenly begin to clamor—a completely unexpected reaction, as far as Burke was concerned. As he approached, he realized that Angel Paredes, although short, didn't really seem to be. She seemed larger than life to him. Maybe because he'd read so many of her mission reports.

More than anything, he liked her large, dark brown eyes, which seem to glimmer like a moonlit night. They were slightly tilted, giving her an exotic look he hadn't expected. Her face was broad, her eyes wide set, with a fine, straight nose that gave her an aristocratic look. She was probably no more than five foot six, Burke realized, towering over her from his own six-foot height. His gaze dropped to her mouth—a lush, full mouth, the corners tucked upward, indicating she laughed a lot.

He liked her. More than he should, he realized. She was exotic. Mysterious. And in the Peruvian army, presently on loan to the U.S. Army. An eclectic mixture that drew Burke strongly. Instantly, he slammed the door on his heart's interest. His personal feelings had no place in this formula. Nor did his burning curiosity to know everything about her.

Angel looked up into Gifford's craggy, cold features as he approached. The sight of him in civilian clothes—a pair of well-worn Levi's and a dark blue polo shirt that clearly outlined his powerful chest and firmly muscled body—made her gulp. Why on earth was she being drawn to him like this? Was it his cool gray eyes, assessing her like a predator might its quarry? That mouth, so thinned in the picture, but now relaxed and surprisingly strong? In person, this man had dynamic charisma, something that hadn't been obvious in his photo.

Tensing, Angel felt her pulse race erratically. He moved like a jaguar, his body lean and tight. He missed nothing with those alert eyes of his. She saw his gaze flit around, felt him absorbing the energy and atmosphere of the cave and the ops activity going on around him. Her own radar was working flawlessly, and she sensed he was curious and eager. His curiosity made her feel a little too vulnerable at the moment.

Two days ago, she'd injured her tendon once again in a silly movement. This time, Elizabeth put her arm in a sling to protect her from herself while it healed. Though she was relatively pain free, so long as she didn't move her arm much, Angel hadn't expected to be overwhelmed by this Special Forces guy. But she was. And he was approaching her far too quickly for her to make sense of the array of feelings and sensations moving through her. Confused, Angel tried to pretend she was at ease and casual.

"Sergeant Paredes? I'm Burke Gifford." He stopped and held out his hand to her.

"Welcome to BJS, Sergeant." Angel proffered her own. His hand was large, lightly furred with dark brown hair on the back and thick calluses on the palm, along with a lot of small scars here and there. Gulping, she slid her much smaller hand into his, hoping he wouldn't give her a bone-crushing shake. He didn't. To her surprise, Gifford monitored the amount of pressure he exerted. He knew she had a shoulder injury, and simply squeezed her damp fingers warmly before releasing them. That implied he had some sensitivity. That was good.

"Thanks. This is quite an operation. I'm really impressed. I had no idea...." Burke liked, too much, the feel of her strong, soft hand in his. Her fingers were cool and damp. Was she nervous? He perused her upturned face. She was arrestingly attractive in that exotic way. Sternly, he told himself he shouldn't care what Angel looked like. He was here on a scouting mission. To learn from her. That was *all*.

Angel nearly jerked her hand away when wild tingles started running up her hand, jolting her. Surprising her. She saw his straight dark brows gather at her obvious reaction.

"Thanks, Sergeant." Quickly, Angel tucked her hand into the pocket of her coat, her fingers burning like fire itself. Stymied, she said, "Let's go to the mess hall. They got hot coffee brewin' and it's a lot warmer in there than it is out here." Even though the temperature was hovering in the low fifties, for Angel, who was acclimatized to the tropics, it was cold.

"Sure, a cup of coffee sounds great," he answered with enthusiasm. Burke fell into step at her side, feeling giddy, elated and excited, in spite of his resolution to keep his emotions in check. Because she was short, he slowed his stride to match hers.

Looking around as they walked toward the back of the cave, Burke shook his head. "This is an incredible facility." There were a number of Quonset huts set in the back of the cave. To one side, he saw the mouth of a tunnel, disappearing off into the mountain. Battery-powered golf carts carrying supplies and personnel zoomed in and out of it like bees from a hive. The clinks and clanks of crews working on Apache gunships and two Blackhawks echoed through the area. Everywhere he looked, he saw women. Only once did he spot a couple of men working with an otherwise all-women flight crew.

Looking down, he studied Angel's strong profile. From this angle, she reminded him of Incan reliefs he'd seen carved in stone. He wondered how personal to get with her. Tamping down his desire to ask her a hundred personal questions, he cautioned himself to go slow and let her open up to him—or not, as the case may be. Inwardly, Burke hoped she would. He was dying to know more about the woman, the person, on whom this legend was based.

Approaching the door to the mess hall, Burke opened it for her out of habit. He saw her look up at him, her eyes narrow briefly, and then a sour smile touch her lips.

"Thanks," she said as she entered.

"You're down one arm," he said. "I thought opening a door for you wouldn't make a gender statement."

Grinning, Angel moved on into the warm facility. When he came to her side and stood patiently, she looked up and said, "We're a pretty independent lot down here, Sergeant. My left arm might be in a sling, but I still have a good right arm that can open doors, too.''

"I'll remember that, Sergeant Paredes."

Angel heard the wry tone in his voice and saw the glimmer of humor in his gray eyes, too. She turned her attention to the chow hall. The long rows of picnic tables were nearly deserted now that breakfast was over. A few pilots on duty, dressed in black flight uniforms, were huddled at one table over a last cup of coffee, but that was about it.

"Hungry, Sergeant?"

"Yeah, I am." He rubbed his belly. "The flight down here served food that would kill a dog. I didn't eat much."

Chuckling, Angel pointed to the line of aluminum trays at one end of the table. "I haven't had breakfast yet, either, so let's belly up to the bar."

Burke did not make the mistake of rushing ahead to get her a tray. He reminded himself of what she'd said—that she had one good hand to work with. Allowing Angel to precede him, he saw two women cooks, dressed in white, with white caps on their heads, waiting to dish up whatever they wanted from the warming trays in the chow line.

Angel was trying to balance her tray and curse her injured arm simultaneously. After her outburst about him opening the door for her, she figured she'd better ante up and do this by herself. She didn't like feeling weak or inept. But the tray was getting heavier as the cooks piled on fluffy scrambled eggs, four pieces of whole wheat toast, a rasher of bacon and some citrus fruit.

Reaching the other end of the line, Angel chose a table and set the tray down before she dropped it and embarrassed herself. Gifford's tray was piled three times as high as hers. Once he reached the table and set it opposite hers, she pointed to the coffee and tea dispenser at the end of the cooks' line.

"We get our java here." Angel went over, grabbed a thick white mug and held it under the appropriate nozzle. When Gifford followed and stood nearby, it made her nervous. He was like a big shadow looming over her, she wasn't used to someone dogging her heels like that. Filling her coffee cup, she quickly stepped away and went back to the table.

As she did, Angel noticed the women pilots covertly watching Gifford. She saw the looks on their faces and grinned to herself. He *was* good-looking, in a rough kind of way. Well, it never hurt to look, did it? Sitting down, she poured cream and sugar into her cup. When Gifford sat down opposite her, her pulse raced momentarily.

"Smells real good. Better than regular army chow," he said with a grin. Picking up his fork, he dived into the scrambled eggs.

Angel ate delicately, studying Burke between bites. He ate like a hungry wolf. She liked his short, neatly cut hair. His ears were large and flared away from his skull slightly. All the better to hear with, she was sure. He had a large Adam's apple and his neck was thick and strong. His broad shoulders made Angel think that this man could carry a lot of responsibility very easily.

She decided that she needed to take the lead, because he was basically a guest on the base. Over the course of the meal, she shared with him why he was here: to be her hands when she needed them. Blushing a bit as she told him how she'd injured her shoulder, she saw him smile fully for the first time. It was a boyish smile, relaxed and unguarded, and as Gifford's icy expression melted away, she was privy to the man beneath the facade. The enormity of the change surprised her, and again she felt confused by the array of feelings just looking at him produced in her heart.

"I've never had tendonitis," Burke said with sympathy, slathering strawberry jam over one of the pieces of toast on his tray. "Broke my ankle in a parachute jump, though."

"I broke my ankle once, too," Angel said, "though not in a chute jump. I can tell you the pain in a tendon is worse than a break."

Nodding, Burke said, "I've treated my share of them off and on through the years, and every guy that had it told me the pain was enough to make you pass out."

"It is," Angel murmured, "and I did." She was finished with breakfast and pushed her tray aside, then picked up her coffee cup. "I sure don't like being down one arm. It cramps my high-flyin' style."

Burke liked her rank sense of humor. He'd never met a paramedic who didn't have a blistering, sardonic wit. "You don't strike me as a woman who takes kindly to being in prison."

Giving him a skeptical look, Angel studied him. Gifford had a soft Southern drawl. "Man or woman, no one likes prison, don't you think?"

"I guess I didn't say that right," he stated, taking a second piece of toast and slathering it with jam. "You strike me as the kind of person who likes her freedom and bucks any boundaries or fences folks might try to put around her."

Nodding, Angel said, "I see. Yeah, I'm like that,

I guess." Burke had a disturbing ability to see right through her. That made her antsy.

"I don't know about the Peruvian army, but in the U.S. Army it's nice having the freedom to do what you're best at."

Sipping the coffee, Angel said, "Well, it's a little different down here if a woman wants to join the male military organization."

"A lot of prejudice against you, gender-wise?"

"Tons of it."

Burke studied her. He saw that her eyes were hooded, guarded against him. Sensing that she was feeling him out, that she really wasn't comfortable around him yet, he asked, "Does it bother you that I'm a man walkin' in on your turf?"

"Excuse me?"

He lifted his hand. "This is a women's black ops. I didn't see too many men as I came through the complex. There must be a reason for it."

Frowning, Angel growled, "I don't know how much you know about the Black Jaguar Squadron, but yes, it was created because of gender prejudice, for sure. By the trouble some female officers had with the white boys up there at Fort Rucker. Major Stevenson was in the first all-women Apache pilot training program there. The women pilots suffered a lot at the hands of the men. Captain York, the

chief instructor, washed out a number of good student pilots because he didn't want women in
Apaches. He didn't feel they had the goods to handle the job.'' Derision filled Angel's tone as she
glared across the table at Gifford. ''Well, Lieutenant Stevenson didn't take the gender prejudice crap
lying down. She fought back within the student program as well as afterward. Luckily, her father is a
general in the army. When she came to him with
her proposal for this black ops you have the privi-
lege of sitting in right now, Sergeant, he made it
happen. Maya Stevenson was not going to let the
survivors of that hell on earth at Fort Rucker be
destroyed by male prejudice.''

Angel looked around, anger in her tone, her
words tight and biting. ''She had a vision. She
wanted a place where women could be fostered and
nurtured to bring out their best. She wanted an un-
prejudiced environment for all, so we could perform
at our best. She gathered women from many military branches from many different countries, in-
cluding Peru, which is how I got transferred here
to BJS. When the squadron moved down here, a lot
of army brass laughed behind their backs. But that
was okay, because Maya knew we could do it.
There were plenty of bets placed on all sides that
we'd fail. But we didn't. We not only survived,

we've thrived. Now, nearly four years later, Major Stevenson has proved herself and her program. Now the U.S. Army is standing in line to get its male pilots, ground crews and people like you down here to take advantage of our hard-won knowledge.'' Nostrils flaring, Angel eyed him sharply. ''So yeah, we're a little prickly about men comin' down here. It's not that we don't like them, it's that they tend to see us as the weaker sex, incapable of doing the same things they do—as well or better.'' She spat out the last two words.

''I didn't mean to suggest there *should* be more men here....''

''Really? Coulda fooled me, Sergeant.'' Her voice was cool. Grinding.

''I just didn't know how the Black Jaguar Squadron came into existence.''

She saw the pained look on Burke's face as he held up his large, square hands—a sign of truce. She sipped her coffee, which was scaldingly hot and matched her anger. Setting the cup down with finality, she growled, ''Do me a favor, Sergeant? I really don't like having you dog my heels. It's not my thing to have someone hanging around me like a ball and chain. You have a job to do—you're my hands. When I need your help, I'll ask. Otherwise, take the position of listening and learning. Got it?''

Surprised at the anger in her voice, Burke sat there calmly, adjusting to the unexpected attack. Obviously, he'd hit a sore point with Paredes. But he realized he'd better clean up his language and the way he said things or he was going to be in hot water more times than not. And not only with her. This was a woman-commanded facility, for the most part.

"Yeah, I got it, Sergeant Paredes. I meant no disrespect."

"No man ever does. It just happens."

Feeling like an outsider, or as if he were an alien male come to an all-female world, Burke sat there in silence. He had six weeks here. All of a sudden, the assignment felt like a prison to him. The exotic-looking Angel Paredes seemed more like an avenging angel right now. In his heart, he was saddened by how things were turning out. She was incredibly beautiful, in such an arresting way, that Burke was having a helluva time keeping his heart out of this chaotic equation.

"I think," he told her in a low and apologetic tone, "that I can learn a lot about prejudice from you in the next six weeks. It's something the army is trying to rectify daily with classes, to help us recognize that women are equals."

Snorting, Angel stood up. "Equals? We're *better*

than any man, in my book. And this isn't some academic statement, Sergeant Gifford. It's spoken from hard-earned experience in the field. Frankly, I wish you were a woman. It would make this six weeks a lot easier on both of us.''

Chapter Three

When he learned that he was staying in the TDY Quonset hut—a place where temporary duty personnel were housed—Burke went there to change. His room was small, spare and simple. This was a no-frills gig, but that didn't bother him. At least he had a bunk to sleep on and hot water to shower and shave with. After getting into his uniform, which consisted of a pair of jungle fatigues, a dark green T-shirt, black boots and a black baseball cover with a BJS patch on it, Burke met Angel over at the dispensary.

Shaking off the exhaustion of the flight, he tried

to steel himself for the prickly but exotic Sergeant Paredes. As he walked across the uneven black surface of the cave floor, he once again marveled at how large the compound was. Around him, women personnel worked swiftly and tirelessly, loading ammunition on board the Apaches, or performing maintenance on them. The two workhorses, the Blackhawk helicopters, sat farther back in the complex, behind the gunships, and he saw that one was being loaded with supplies as he made his way to his destination.

Letting his thoughts return to Angel, Burke scowled. Where had he gone wrong with her? He didn't like the fact that they were getting off on the wrong foot with one another. She was really defensive, and didn't like men for some reason. She could have had an experience or series of experiences that made her feel that way.

Great. Well, that didn't help him, did it? Slowing his pace, Burke opened the door to the Quonset hut that had Dispensary painted in red on it.

As he entered, familiar smells of alcohol, bleach and other cleansing agents greeted him. He saw a tall red-haired woman in a white lab coat, stethoscope around her neck, sitting at a green military desk at one end, filling out paperwork. She was tall, with a narrow face. Closing the door, Burke said, "Ma'am? Are you Dr. Elizabeth Cornell?"

She smiled. "Yes, I am." Putting down her pen and shoving away from her desk, Elizabeth stood and walked toward him. "Angel said you were coming over, Sergeant Gifford. Welcome to BJS."

The doctor's hand was long and lean, appropriate for a surgeon, Burke thought, as he took it. He liked her large, warm green eyes. "Yes, ma'am, that's me. Where's Sergeant Paredes?" he asked as he released her hand.

"Oh, in the back, in supply. She's off-duty for the next six weeks, but is helping me out anyway. We just got in a bunch of IVs and other medical equipment, and she's putting it away." Elizabeth smiled a little. "She's experiencing a lot of frustration at the moment being one-armed. I think you'd better go back there and help her out."

"Be glad to," Burke lied. It would be like going into a room with a pissed off, cornered cougar. Walking through the door, he entered a clean and brightly lit room. Seeing Angel down on her knees, putting away the bulky IV kits, he came over to her.

"Need some help?"

"No," Angel muttered when she realized Gifford was standing above her as she struggled to put away the supplies. The shelf for IVs was on the bottom, and the kits needed to be filed by size. But IV kits were bulky and awkward to handle. Ordinarily, Angel had no problem with them. Ordinarily, she had two hands to wrestle them neatly into stacks. However, working with one arm was making her frustrated—and irritable.

Burke hunkered down beside her. "Sure?"

"Damned sure."

"I thought I was supposed to be your hands for you while you rested up," he said as lightly as possible.

"You are when I ask you to be," she said, gritting her teeth. There! Finally, the stubborn IV slid into place. Awkwardly, Angel straightened up. Pushing the hair off her face with her good hand, she glared up at Gifford. His mask was back on, but she saw the look in his eyes; it was one of concern for her. She saw compassion for her plight, too, and that threw her. After their earlier clash with one another, she'd thought he'd be prickly as hell and ready to carry a grudge.

"How can I help you then?" Burke asked, looking at the unopened cardboard boxes that littered the center of the room—the same ones that had been flown in with him earlier on the Bell helicopter.

"Why don't you go ask Dr. Liz if she needs your help?"

"Okay." He rose, turned around and left. The door shut behind him.

"Alone. Good." Angel crawled over to the next box. The tape across the top had to be cut. Grabbing the knife, she stabbed at the tape, but the box slid away across the highly polished, white-tiled floor. Without two hands, she couldn't hold it in place. The knife blade pierced the cardboard and got stuck.

"Let go!" Angel snarled, yanking at the knife.

The door opened.

Just as the blade became unstuck, a pain shot through Angel's sensitive left shoulder. The shock was like a cold electrical current. Gasping, she released the blade and it went flying out of her hand.

Burke ducked as the knife sailed past his head and slammed into the door beside him. Glass shattered, sprinkling over him and the surrounding area.

Eyes widening, Angel gasped again as she cradled her left elbow with her right hand. If Gifford hadn't moved as fast as he had, the knife would have hit him. Gulping, she sat there in the middle of the floor, feeling completely embarrassed.

"That was close," Burke murmured with a slight grin. He saw the shock and humiliation in Angel's face. Somehow, he wanted to let her know it was okay, that he knew it was an accident.

"I didn't mean it—"

"I know that," he soothed. Turning, he opened the door. One of the panes had been shattered.

Elizabeth stuck her head around the door. "Angel?"

"Aww, the knife just slipped out of my hand, Doc."

"Everyone okay?" She looked at them worriedly.

"Yeah," Angel mumbled. "I'm fine."

"No injuries," Burke told her. "It was an accident...."

"Okay." Elizabeth frowned. "Angel, why don't you let the sergeant help you? I have nothing for him to do, and getting these supplies logged in is the most important activity right now."

"Yeah...okay," she muttered, defeated.

Burke looked around and found a small broom and a dustpan. He went about collecting the glass shards, pouring them into the wastebasket in the corner. Glancing toward Angel as he dumped the last pan, he saw the humiliation in her face. What could he say to her that wouldn't make her more angry? Or defensive? Unsure, he put the broom and dustpan away.

"How's the pain in that left shoulder? Pretty intense?"

Glumly, Angel looked up as Gifford squatted down in front of her, his long, lean hands dangling between his opened thighs. The expression on his face had thawed, and she saw his concern. Biting down on her lower lip, she mumbled, "Yeah, I was trying to open that box over there. I musta moved the wrong way, because I got such a sharp pain down my left arm, it surprised me."

Looking around, Burke said quietly, "Want me to slit them open?"

"I guess...." Brows flattening, Angel decided she was saddled with this guy whether she liked it or not. "Go ahead, open them all."

Burke nodded and slowly rose. He retrieved the errant knife and began to open the boxes, one after another. Angel pulled one toward where she was kneeling, to start to put the contents away, but before she knew it, Gifford had opened all twenty cartons and was handing the knife back to her.

"Can I put any of the stuff away?" he asked, pointing to the various-size dressings and bandages it contained.

"Yeah, over there, up on that shelf," Angel said quietly, gesturing to a row of green metal shelves along the other wall. Relieved that he was going to take a box other than the one she was working on, she gave a little sigh.

Taking his time, Burke began to familiarize himself with how the supply area was laid out. It was obvious Angel didn't want him anywhere near her. Too tired to try and think his way out of a paper bag at this point, Burke settled for distant civility from her. Militarily, Angel was the same rank as he, though she was in the Peruvian army instead of the U.S. one. In a sense, Burke was glad of the common ground, because if one of them had a higher rank, especially him, it would have probably added more fuel to the conflagration between them. And then everything would have gone to hell in a handbasket, as his pa would have said. Not that it hadn't already. How could he save what was left of their tattered relationship? Burke didn't know at this point. He felt as if he was walking on land mines every minute with Angel. She might have a wonderful name, but in his eyes she was acting like a devil.

"Tell me about your people," Burke said casually as he stocked the shelves. "I didn't get much of a briefing on you before I left. I'd like to try and understand so I don't keep setting off land mines between us."

Giving him a dark look, Angel hesitated. She was

standing on the opposite side of the room, putting away syringes. "Are you familiar with the Incas?" Over the years, she had found that North Americans really weren't up on history, especially involving anyone outside their own country. She found that amazing. World history had been a very important part of her own education.

"Not really."

"Thought so."

"Excuse me?" Burke twisted to look over his shoulder, his hand poised in midair. Seeing the scowl on Angel's face, he wondered what she was so upset about now.

"How much history did you have in school, Sergeant?"

"Not much."

"That's my point. I find *norteamericanos* sadly lacking in knowledge of anyone but themselves."

"You're right," Burke said, putting the dressings away. "We need to widen our horizon to include everyone else." Giving her a brief smile, he said, "So enlighten me, will you? I'm all ears."

That slight, boyish smile he gave her, stunned Angel. For a moment, Gifford's face had magically transformed again. The sight left her breathless. And interested in ways she didn't want to be.

Taking a steadying breath, she began. "The Inca

Empire stretched from Ecuador down through Chile at one time. The Incas' descendants—my people—are called the Quero. We speak a language known as Quechua. The Quero live in scattered communities across Peru. There aren't many of us left, and those that are left are looked down upon like rats or something worse by descendants of the Spanish people who conquered us.''

"More prejudice," he murmured, realizing that some of her prickliness might be due to how other Peruvians viewed her and her people.

"Yeah, for sure." Angel bent and picked up another box of syringes. "My village is in Rainbow Valley, above Agua Caliente. The Quero are farming people. We live *with* the land, not on it. Our belief system formed the underpinnings of the entire Inca Empire."

"Which is?"

"What religion are you, Sergeant?"

"Protestant. Why?"

"Well, by your standards, I'm a pagan," Angel said with a savage grin. "Years ago I would have probably been burned at the stake, because my belief system is an earth-centered one." She pointed down at the floor. "You know about Mother Earth. My people believe we're all related and connected, and that everything comes from her."

"I see." Burke turned and folded up the box he'd emptied, then placed it in the corner. Moving to another box near Angel, he took a risk and sat down about six feet away from her. "My pa is part Choctaw Indian, even though he goes to a Protestant church with my mother," he said. "I grew up hearing a lot of Choctaw stories, so I'm sort of familiar with what you're talking about."

"Well," Angel said darkly, "at least you've got *some* Indian blood runnin' through your veins."

"Is that good?"

She managed a sour smile. "To me, it is. Indians are Indians. Full- or part-blood doesn't matter."

"What does it mean to you?" he asked, folding his hands in his lap.

"Blood is memory, Sergeant. Through it our ancestors speak to us, from the past into our present."

"You can call me Burke if you want." He held out the offer like a tentative olive branch. Perhaps the fact that he had Choctaw blood in him would help her open up more to him. He saw her sit back on her heels, studying him with her intense brown eyes, her lips compressed as she considered his request.

"Yeah...well, okay...but continue to call me Paredes or Sergeant."

"Great. How about a coffee break? Or do you

get those around here?'' he asked wryly. ''I'm about twenty-four hours without sleep and I want to keep going today and crash tonight.''

''Oh…'' Angel felt foolish. She was being very self-centered right now. Overly so. Why hadn't she considered that the sergeant—Burke—had had a long, hard flight and was probably sleep-deprived? If he'd been a woman, Angel would have instantly considered that possibility. Angry with herself, she realized she was being prejudiced toward him because he was a man. Well, men weren't exactly stellar in her universe, anyway—and it had taken five long years for her to get over the last man she'd allowed herself to love. At that time, Angel had sworn she'd never tangle with another one. The pain of lost love was too much to ever bear twice.

''Er, sure. We can take a break. Let's go.'' She quickly scrambled to her feet, her right hand beneath her left elbow to stabilize her shoulder.

''Music to my ears,'' Burke said to her, slowly unwinding in turn. Dusting off his knees and the seat of his pants, he followed Angel to the door. He didn't make the mistake of trying to open it this time, letting her do it, instead.

Angel gave the gaping hole in the door a sad look. ''I gotta get someone over here to fix that,'' she muttered, more to herself than to him. At the front of the dispensary, she saw the doctor still working on paperwork at her desk.

"We're gonna take a break, Liz."

"Fine. You okay, Angel? Is the pain in your arm still bad?"

"No, I'm okay. I just made too quick a movement. I'm still learning how to cope with this." She grinned apologetically at the doctor.

Elizabeth chuckled. "Give yourself some latitude, Angel. It's gonna take forty-eight hours for most of the pain to dissipate after that shot I gave you the other day, okay? Let Sergeant Gifford help you."

"I am," she said grimly, opening the outer door.

Burke walked at Angel's shoulder as they headed back to the mess hall. It was noon, and there was a lot more activity around the Quonset hut. The ring of female laughter and chatter was everywhere.

"This sounds like a pretty happy place," he murmured. Unable to help himself, Burke slanted a glance down at Angel's profile. Her lips had been pursed. When he'd made the comment, they softened. She had a beautiful mouth. Gorgeous. Too gorgeous, as far as he was concerned.

"Major Stevenson is a wild woman in disguise. She runs BJS the way she thinks it should be run." Angel opened her hand and looked up at Burke.

His eyes were darker and there was a smoldering quality to them that took her off guard. It was a look a man gave a woman he was interested in. Instantly, Angel's heart pounded—with dread, with euphoria. Confused, she asked, "Why are you looking at me like that?"

Burke slowed to a halt, as did Angel, leaving a few feet between them. He'd been caught red-handed. But then, no woman had ever challenged him on his desires. Honesty was the best policy. "I saw your mouth relax, instead of being bunched in a thin line." He hesitated. "I think you have a beautiful mouth when you're not uptight." *Ouch,* he thought as Angel's eyes narrowed speculatively.

"That didn't exactly come out right, did it?" he offered apologetically.

"No…it didn't."

"Are you upset about me thinking you have a beautiful mouth or for thinking that you're uptight?" He saw her eyes widen, and then her mouth curved into a devilish grin. Relief swept through Burke.

"How about I let you sweat this one out and figure it out for yourself, Sergeant?"

Burke had no one to blame but himself. "Looks like I need more sensitivity-training classes."

"Looks like. Come on, I'm hungry." Angel

turned and strode quickly toward the mess. Her heart was pounding and she felt shaky. She had a beautiful mouth! At least Burke thought so. No man had ever said that about her. The compliment had been real; she'd seen the sincerity in Burke's stormy-looking eyes and in the way he'd opened his hands toward her while trying to explain himself. Shaking her head, she decided the man had more foot-in-mouth disease than most males had.

Put in his place, Burke stood in the chow line with about ten other women, Angel in front of him. He noticed a lot of glances, sizing him up. Some seemed admiring, others, like Angel's, guarded and circumspect. The noise level in the hall was high, with laughter, teasing and joking going on constantly as the female personnel ate lunch at their respective tables.

The fried chicken, dumplings and salad looked surprisingly good. Burke thanked the two women cooks, who both blushed furiously at his sincere compliments. Following Angel to a table that had just been vacated by four women pilots in black flight uniforms, he sat down opposite her and said, "Coffee?"

"Er, yeah…" Angel had forgotten to get it.

"Stay there," Burke said, holding out his hand.

"I'll fetch you a cup." And then he hesitated. "Unless I'm out of line?"

Grinning, Angel shook her head. "Naw, go ahead."

As he walked away, she tried to ignore how tall, strong and confident he was. Just as she was going to bite into a drumstick, Snow Queen, one of the pilots, came over and bent down near her ear.

"Where did you get that hunk, Angel? Me and the girls at the other table are salivating over him. Is he married? Got a million kids? Divorced? What? We wanna know."

Glancing up at the red-haired pilot, whose green eyes were filled with humor, Angel frowned. "Gimme a break, will you? He just got here a couple of hours ago."

"We noticed you didn't seem too taken with him. Is it open season?"

Angel knew what *that* comment meant. If she wasn't interested personally in Burke, provided all signals were "go" and he wasn't married, another one of the enlisted women had her eye on him—already.

"What is this? A man-hungry squadron?"

Snow Queen chortled and squeezed her right arm gently. "Listen, three and a half years without hardly a man around here have left all of us like horny, slavering wolves. Anything on two legs that's male gets our attention. There's still not enough guys in the squadron as far as we're concerned.''

Giving her a sour grin, Angel said, ''Gimme some time, will you? We're not exactly getting along. So far, the situation's touchy.''

''Umm, okay. Well, just to let you know, my crew chief, Tess Fairbanks, has her eye on him.''

Groaning, Angel twisted to look at the table behind here, where Tess sat eating with the rest of Snow Queen's ground crew. Tess was a tall, lanky Kentucky gal with light brown hair, aqua-blue eyes and a wide, easy grin. She lifted her hand and did a thumbs-up in Angel's direction. Angel gave her a thumbs-down.

''Okay,'' Snow Queen said, straightening. ''Your guy is comin' back so I'm skedaddling. Just keep us updated on this situation, huh?'' She grinned and left.

Burke saw the woman pilot leave Angel's side as he approached. Angel was scowling again, biting into a drumstick like a wolf biting the hand that fed it. ''Here you go.''

Wiping her mouth with a paper napkin, Angel muttered, ''Thanks…''

Getting situated, Burke gave her a conspiratorial

look. He leaned over, his voice low. "Is this normal?"

"What?"

"All the women staring at me?"

"How's it feel? Now you know how a woman feels when she goes by a group of men who start callin' and whistling and embarrassing her."

Raising his brows, Burke leaned back and began to eat. "I thought it was kind of nice."

"You're a man. You would."

"Tell me something?"

"Maybe."

"Do you hate men?"

"No. I just don't like that most of them have their brains between their legs. You can't think your way out of a paper bag with that kind of anatomy."

Burke roared with laughter. His male voice, deep and rolling, momentarily broke through the feminine chatter in the mess. Every single woman stopped talking, lifted her head and looked in their direction.

Angel cringed. She bit down hard on the chicken leg. Though she tried to ignore the looks of her squad mates, she could have killed Gifford for his laughter. Of course, he had a nice laugh, if she was honest with herself. And his entire face changed— remarkably. He was actually quite good-looking when he smiled. Unhappy with her response to him, she snapped, "I just insulted you."

"No, you called that one. I'm finding out you like a fast game of tit for tat. I'm okay with that, insults and all. In fact, I'm ready, willing and able to go head-to-head with you."

"Don't flatter yourself too much, Gifford."

"With you around, I won't have to, will I? You'll keep me in line."

He gave her a big, loose smile, both his elbows on the table, bracketing his tray.

"You're really full of yourself. You know that?"

"Probably," he admitted candidly. "But you're no soft-boiled egg, either."

"What's that supposed to mean?"

"Well," Burke said, "it means you're a woman who's been around, and you know how to roll with the punches. I like a gal who's strong and confident like your are."

"Two compliments in a row. I can hardly stand it."

"I'm on a roll, don't you think?"

"Please."

"Well, it's better than the alternative, right?"

"What's the alternative?"

"Insults."

"Oh, those. I dole them out regularly."

"I know."

Giving him a flat look, Angel could see he was teasing her. And she was teasing back. It felt good. For the first time in five years, her heart was feeling light—for no discernible reason.

"I read your file. You're a redneck from Arkansas. Men from that area don't honor women. They look *down* on them. And that's not gonna happen between you and me. I've had a gutful of that down here in Peru before I was assigned to BJS."

"Whoa…" Burke wiped his mouth with his napkin and set it aside. "I've never looked down on you, Sergeant. And I'm not about to. Remember? I'm the one who spent six months trying to get down here to meet you? To talk to you? You're a legend in the U.S. Army. They say you've saved lives that should have expired—lots of 'em. I've read all your debriefs on missions you've flown." He shrugged and gave her an intense look. "And by all rights, those people should have died."

Feeling uncomfortable, Angel muttered, "With your religious background, you wouldn't believe what happened, anyway. So I think you're barking up the wrong tree."

"Now, that's a good coon-dog saying." Burke cocked his head and smiled fully. "You know, for having been born here in Peru, you have American slang down pat. Have you been to the U.S.?''

''No. The pilots taught it to me. They're real wild women.''

''If I didn't know better, hearing you speak such flawless English, I'd never think you were Incan.''

''I'm Quero. We don't call ourselves Incas anymore.''

''That's a shame because I was thinking earlier that from the profile of your face, you remind me of some of the carved stone reliefs I've seen pictured in magazines. In articles on the Inca civilization.''

''That's the third compliment.''

''Is there a maximum allowed?''

''Gifford, you're such a BS artist.''

''No, not really. I'm honest.''

''An honest man.'' The words came out with clear derision. ''Yeah, right.'' Angel stabbed at the vegetables on her tray.

Burke said nothing because he realized he'd noticed how pain filled Angel's eyes at his last comment. He had no wish whatsoever to inflict pain on her. He wondered if she might someday share why she was so dismissive of a man's ability to be honest.

Chapter Four

As Angel entered the Blackhawk helicopter, she clambered between the boxes that had been anchored to the deck of the helo with nylon cargo netting. Three days had passed since Gifford had landed at BJS and become her shadow. Even as she made her way over to the nylon seat where she'd stay for the duration of their flight, she knew he'd be boarding momentarily and on her heels once more. With her bum left arm in a sling, a part of her was glad he was there to help out. The other part of her was irritated by his constant nearness.

Angel tried to keep her ire to herself, but didn't always manage to.

Sticking her head into the cockpit, she saw Snake and Wild Woman at the controls. Outside, the ground crew was getting ready to push the helo out on the lip so they could start the engines.

"Lucky me. I've got the two of you," Angel said.

Wild Woman glanced back as she strapped herself into the copilot's seat, on the left. "Hey, we got the hunk! Snake and I are slobbering all over ourselves up here. Lucky you, Angel!"

Angel snorted. "You can have 'im."

"Ah, shucks," wailed Snake, who sat in the pilot's seat. "Enlisteds and officers don't mix."

That was true, Angel conceded. "You can look—just don't touch, ladies."

Snake chortled as she wrapped the knee board around her right thigh with its Velcro strap and situated it in place. "Oh, yeah, we can look and dream."

"I think every woman in the squadron envies you," Wild Woman said as she began flipping a series of switches on the console between them.

With a frown, Angel saw Gifford boarding. Today he was dressed in civilian clothes, as she was. They were heading out to a Quero village fifty miles south of them, Yanatin. It was a trip the crew made once a month, to provide medical assistance to the farming families that lived there.

"I'd give anything to be doin' this alone."

Wild Woman laughed. "Angel, you're just too used to being without a man around. Hey, he seems pretty nice, from what we can tell. And Doc was saying he's a good dude."

"Doc isn't saddled with him twelve hours a day," Angel growled.

"Well, strap in," Snake told her with a laugh. "We're ready to rock 'n' roll."

"Yeah, right…" Angel turned and went back to her seat at the rear of the cargo hold. Gifford was already sitting in his seat, leaving about a foot of space between them.

Burke saw the unhappy look on Angel's face as she stepped carefully between the supplies. He knew that look was there because of him. In the last three days, Angel had more or less accepted him in her life, but she wasn't thrilled about it. Her comment about an "honest man" stuck with him. Intuitively, he understood he'd hit a raw nerve with Angel. Who had lied to her in the past?

As Angel made her way to her seat, one of the ground crew slid the door shut and locked it. Without the daylight pouring in the cabin was darker.

Burke watched discreetly as Angel fumbled with her good hand to arrange the lap belt across her thighs. Refraining from asking if she needed help, he let her struggle on her own. She was highly independent and wouldn't appreciate his help.

The helo jerked slightly and then began to roll as the cart, hooked up to the nosewheel, began to push the craft gently toward the lip for takeoff. Burke reached for a set of headphones that hung behind him on the metal bulkhead. Placing them on his ears, he could immediately hear the chatter of the pilots. Sliding a glance to his left, he saw that Angel had finally gotten the lap belt on, strapped snugly in place over her thighs.

He saw her look at the set of earphones hanging nearby. There was a look of frustration on her face. With her left arm in the sling, she couldn't reach them. Burke thought about asking if she'd like some help, but resisted.

Anger bubbled in Angel. She hated being without her left arm! It was the most pulverizing experience that could have happened to her. An inflamed tendon, of all things! Damn, she wanted those earphones on, the mike close to her lips so she could chat with Snake and Wild Woman. It was so much fun teasing them and sharing laughter and stories with them. In order to get it, she'd have to have help.

Gritting her teeth, she turned to Burke, who was watching her through hooded eyes. "Can you get those headphones for me? Please?"

Burke nodded. "No problem." Reaching out, he lifted them off the hook and handed them to Angel.

"Thanks." Putting the headset on with one hand was awkward, and she messed up her hair in the process. But after a few moments, Angel managed to settle them in place. Pulling the black microphone close to her lips, she turned the headset on.

"We're hot?" Angel asked.

"I think," Wild Woman said. "Sergeant Gifford? You hear us okay?"

"Yes, ma'am, loud and clear."

"Me, too," Snake said, "even though you didn't ask me."

"I would've. You just jumped the gun, Snake. You're always so impatient," the copilot teased.

"Me? Impatient?" Snake demanded. "I'm not the one with a red streak in her hair."

The Blackhawk eased to a halt, now positioned for takeoff. Burke had watched this ritual play out many times in the last few days. The helicopters were all kept safe and sound, within the maw of the cavern. Only when they were going to be used were they pushed to the lip, where the blades were untethered in preparation for takeoff.

"We're free," Wild Woman said, looking out her window at the crew chief, who gave her a thumbs-up.

"Roger. Let's power up," Snake murmured.

Burke always liked riding in helos. He loved the versatile Blackhawk, which could be turned from a war machine into a supply wagon and back again. Today, they were flying to a remote Quero village to bring medical help to the people there. He looked forward to it. Glancing at Angel, he saw she had a clipboard on her lap, which she was studying intently, pen in hand.

He liked looking at her in moments like this, when she wasn't aware that he was staring at her. Oh, he shouldn't be, he knew, but Burke couldn't help himself. The more Angel pushed him away, the law of attraction seemed to kick in, multiplying the attraction he felt exponentially. With his past track record, Burke knew he shouldn't be interested at all in this feisty Quero woman—but he was. And there was the rub: she interested him in so many ways. He was dying to ask her a lot of questions— personal ones—but he knew by now that unless she chose to divulge those delectable pieces of information to him on her own, she would see his questions as an invasion of her privacy.

As he heard the engines start to whine, the blades slowly begin to turn, Burke continued to watch Angel out of the corner of his eye. She was dressed in a pair of well-worn jeans, a red tank top and a dark green canvas jacket. It was the jacket that garnered his interest. There were hand-woven rainbow-colored panels on each shoulder. The thick, black strands of her hair, shining in the low light, lay beautifully against her well-shaped head. And he found himself wanting to slide his fingers through them to find out if her hair was as soft as it looked.

Angel sat with her hands on top of the clipboard as the Blackhawk gently lifted off the lip. Their next maneuver was to fly through the Eye, which was no small feat on the best of days. She glanced at Gifford, who was completely mesmerized as the Blackhawk inched upward and then flew straight for the hole in the lava wall ahead of them.

Angel tried not to like his easy, laid-back Southern ways. He looked devastatingly handsome in the formfitting jeans that outlined his strongly muscled, lean legs. The dark blue polo shirt he wore beneath his camel-colored light wool jacket emphasized the breadth of his chest. No, there was nothing about him not to enjoy, Angel decided.

Once they flew through the Eye and began climbing out of the swirling mists that surrounded the mountain cave complex, bright sunlight lanced through the cabin. Angel absorbed the vibration of the chopper; it was lulling and comforting to her. The noise level was high, however, and without earphones on, no one would be able to communicate.

"What's on the agenda today at the village?" Burke asked her.

"The usual stuff. We'll go into the chief's hut and set up a mobile clinic. Then the villagers will bring their kids, the elderly or themselves for medical attention. We'll be dealing with ear infections, a cut that has to be cleaned out, or other minor emergencies."

He grinned and patted the pocket of his jacket. "I brought along some hard candy for the kids. Can we hand that out to them? For medicinal purposes, of course."

Angel melted beneath his boyish smile. She knew Burke was still searching to somehow establish a positive connection between them. She felt guilty over how she'd treated him. "Candy cures everything," she laughed softly. "Yeah, I always pack away a couple of bags of candy in the supplies.'' She pointed to the boxes beneath the cargo netting in front of them.

"Oh…okay.''

"Hey, it's a great idea you had. A nice gesture. And sensitive, too.…'' she said, then stopped herself. She didn't want to lavish him with compliments.

"When I was over in Somalia, in Mogadishu, we found out the kids loved our rations. They loved the candy bars we had even more.''

Angel blinked. Burke had been in Somalia? Her mind scrambled back to that time frame, and the horrible losses the Army Rangers and Delta Force had suffered in that city run by local warlords. "Somalia?''

"Yeah,'' Burke said, growing serious. He saw surprise and then some other emotion on Angel's face. Respect, maybe. "I was with the medical detachment for the U.S. Army over there, not in Special Forces at that time.''

"Then…'' Angel swallowed hard "…you saw it all.…''

Grimly, Burke nodded. "I saw too much, Angel—er, I mean, Sergeant.'' Damn! He'd blown it. He'd called her by her first name when she'd specifically told him not to. Burke hadn't meant to do that. In his head, he always called her Angel, not by her military designation.

Her name had rolled off his tongue like a caress. Angel blinked twice when he made the slipup. When she saw his face turn a dull red, she realized he was blushing. Holding up her hand, she managed a sour smile. "Relax, I don't eat people for breakfast if they call me by my first name."

Nodding, Burke said, "Thanks, that's good to know." Judging by the sparkle in her dark brown eyes, she wasn't going to be angry over the mistake.

"Most people," Wild Woman informed him archly over the intercom, "call her lots of names. Just depends what scenario is playin' out."

Hearing the laughter of the two women pilots, Burke smiled. He saw Angel grin, too.

"Yeah," Snake informed him drolly, "and most of them aren't printable, much less nice."

"Well," Angel muttered defiantly, "when things get hot and heavy, you two birds aren't exactly Miss Manners, either. In fact Miss Manners would faint dead away, if she saw you two in combat and swearin' a blue streak."

Burke heard the two pilots laugh hilariously in the cockpit. It was interesting to sit in the back. From this angle, he could see through the doorway, so had a view of both women. They were looking at one another, grinning. He decided they had a lot of fun doing what they loved: flying.

"I don't think any of us elevates our language skills very much in a firefight, do we?" Burke murmured.

Angel grinned at him. "Not around here, at least. And those two pilots up there oughta be carrying a bar of soap around with them at all times."

"Ohh," Wild Woman chortled, "you're cruel, Paredes!"

"Watch it," Snake chided, "the Angel of Death has her claws out!"

Everyone laughed, even Burke. For the duration of the trip, their banter ranged over a number of topics, from Russian Kamov Black Shark gunships—which were always a threat to them, even now as they flew toward Yanatin—to politics, to the U.S. Army and candy for the children.

"You know," Angel sighed, "I'd give my other arm for some really good chocolate."

"I'm with you, sister!" Wild Woman exclaimed. "How about Godiva dark chocolate truffles?"

"Naw," Snake growled, "gimme the coconut-filled truffles."

"What kind do you like?" Burke asked Angel.

"Anything that doesn't run the other direction."

Laughter filled the cabin.

"Angel takes no prisoners when it comes to chocolate, Sergeant Gifford," Wild Woman said. "She's our chief chocoholic at the squadron."

"Hell, I'm Incan. We *discovered* chocolate! Gimme a break, will ya? I come by my addiction through my heredity."

"Yep," Snake told Gifford in a conspiratorial tone, "you want to see the Angel of Death smile, just give her a box of chocolates."

"You two birds should be watchin' for Kamovs instead of picking on me about my sweet tooth."

"Oh," Snake said, "you're far more fun to tease."

"You know," Angel said wistfully, "chocolate *does* sound good right now."

Burke smiled at her. She had a soft, yearning look on her face. How he wished he had a box of chocolates to give her.

"Snow Queen's makin' a trip in the civilian helo to Cuzco later today to pick up supplies," Wild Woman noted. "If you're real good, Paredes, we *might* consider asking her to pick you up a box."

Angel laughed. "Oh, and what would I owe you for granting such a favor?"

"Just your firstborn child, is all," Snake replied, giving her a teasing look, a wide smile on her mouth.

"In your dreams, Snake. In your dreams."

Burke didn't know what to make of that comment and decided not to ask. Below them, the jungle was an uneven carpet of greenery, with a canopy of trees of various heights blanketing the hilly landscape. Around them the early morning sky was a pale blue, dotted with puffy clouds in odd, elongated shapes. Ahead, on their right, he could see what he thought was a clearing.

"Get ready for landing," Wild Woman told them. "Yanatin's comin' up."

Burke stood in the large thatched hut that everyone referred to as the meeting place. He'd helped Angel by setting up the folding tables, opening all the boxes and getting things in order. In the meantime, several curious Quero children had come and stood in the doorway, watching them. The village chief, Pedro Augustine, a man in his fifties, had welcomed them with open arms, a wide, almost toothless smile creasing his face. He'd given them coca leaf tea, in a ceremonial welcome to his village.

The line of people outside the hut was long. The village of Yanatin, Angel told him, contained two hundred people. The area around it had been painstakingly cleared hundreds of years earlier to create fields where corn grew to supply the village. It was a healthy, thiving center, from what Burke could see.

Angel handed him a stethoscope, which he put around his neck, then she gave him a pair of latex gloves. She had taken off her jacket because the jungle warmth and humidity were building as the sun rose higher. "You ready?" she asked him.

"As I'll ever be."

"Did you do these kind of clinics in Somalia?"

"Yeah, we did. I'm no stranger to them, but you tell me what you need done and I'll do it."

Nodding, Angel said, "With one hand, I'm not going to manage much."

Seeing the unhappiness in her face, he nodded. "Let me help where I can."

Angel waved her arm toward the door. She spoke in Quechua, the language of her people. Instantly, children tumbled into the hut, making a straggling line to the tables where they stood.

Burke could speak Spanish, and he found out quickly, as he began a careful physical examination of each child who stepped forward, that they could speak it, too. They were shy, beautiful children, with huge brown eyes and soft smiles. After treatment, Angel would hand out a piece of the candy he'd brought to each child in line. Burke suspected this was how she got the kids to come for examinations—with sweets. Soon, mothers started arriving with their babies.

The day sped by. Burke lost track of time. The line finally disappeared around 1500.

"Come on, we make house calls now," Angel informed him. "Bring your medical bag with you."

Picking up the large, red canvas bag, Burke hefted it across his shoulder and followed Angel out into the village. Cooking pots were hung over small fires here and there. Dogs ran around yapping. Children were playing. The women were either knitting, weaving or making meals. Some hunters were returning from the jungle, and Burke spied several of them with a wild pig suspended on a pole between them.

The first hut he and Angel stopped at was near the edge of the village. When she called into the opening, Burke heard a feeble answer.

"Follow me," she told him quietly, stepping into the darkened hut.

Burke allowed his eyes to adjust as Angel moved to a room on the right. As she pulled aside the red woven blanket hanging there, he saw an elderly woman on a dried-grass pallet on the floor. Her gray hair was disheveled and in need of combing. Her skin was nearly the same color as her hair. Halting, he watched as Angel softly greeted her in Quechua and knelt down at her side.

"This is Maria," she told Burke as she settled her hand on the woman's damp forehead. "She's got lung cancer and is dying. There's nothing we can do except give her pain medication and make her as comfortable as possible."

Burke placed the pack on the dirt floor and knelt at the woman's blanketed feet. He saw her dark brown eyes fasten on Angel as she leaned over her. Angel was gently stroking her brow like a mother might a sick child. And then something happened that made Burke think he was hallucinating. As he knelt there watching her lean over Maria, he saw a darkness gather around the upper portion of Angel's body. At first Burke thought he was seeing things. He blinked several times. But the cottony grayness remained. He saw the old woman's eyes close as she sighed and relaxed beneath Angel's hand, which had moved to her upper chest.

Sensing many things, yet unable to understand any of them, Burke saw the woman's face slowly turn from gray to a healthy copper color. He heard Maria sigh, the corners of her toothless mouth turning upward as a slight, trembling smile touched her lips. What was going on?

Everything seemed to grow quiet. The cries of

children playing outdoors faded. So did the barking of the dogs. Burke was excruciatingly aware that the world as he knew it was changing rapidly, due to this one singular experience he was having. But what *was* going on?

Peering through the dimness of the room, he stared intently at Angel's profile. She had her right hand on the woman's upper chest, her eyes closed, her lips slightly parted, and her head was bowed as she knelt at Maria's side. That grayish-black cloud seemed to envelop her entirely now. Burke didn't understand it. He could see the results, however. Maria's skin was flushed and healthy-looking. She seemed to be sleeping deeply and well.

And then Burke began to hear the yapping of the dogs again, and the giggles and laughter of the children seemed to turn up in volume once more. The grayish cloud that had surrounded Angel was dissolving. Staring hard, Burke watched as the cloud completely disappeared. The moment it did, Angel lifted her hand from Maria's chest.

Turning toward Burke, who was staring intently at her, Angel said softly, ''We're done in here. Let's go.'' And then she smiled down at Maria, who continued to sleep peacefully.

Outside, Burke shouldered the medical bag and

walked at Angel's side. "What happened back there?"

"Another form of medicine, Sergeant. One that isn't in those training manuals you write for the U.S. Army. You said in your proposal you wanted to know about these things."

"Hold on." Burke reached out and gently gripped her arm.

Surprised that he'd touched her, Angel halted, her skin tingling pleasantly where his fingers rested on her biceps. Looking up, she saw confusion and curiosity in his gray eyes.

Dropping his hand, Burke said, "Is this the mystery about you? The one I've heard just about everyone back at BJS talk about?"

Shrugging, she said, "I was laying my hands on her. Praying to my spirit guide to send her healing energy, Burke, that's all." Angel inhaled swiftly. She'd called him by his first name! In her present state, all her defenses were down. "I mean, er—"

"I like it when you call me Burke. I'd like to call you Angel, if you would let me."

Standing there, she stared down at her booted feet, thinking about it. "Yeah...okay. That's fine...."

"Good," he said, relief in his tone. "Maybe tonight, when we're back at the base and we aren't busy, we can talk more about what I just saw?''

Angel searched his darkened face. His brow was furrowed, his gaze searching hers. She saw no hint of disbelief in his eyes, as she'd thought she might. ''I don't know if you're ready for the truth, Burke.''

One corner of his mouth pulled upward. ''That's why I came down here, Angel—to find out what *else* you do. How you save lives. I'm never afraid of the truth.''

''Well, you might be this time.''

Chapter Five

Burke noticed that Angel was very quiet and withdrawn on the flight back to base. They landed just before nightfall, as white, wispy clouds closed in over the facility once again. Once they disembarked from the Blackhawk, Burke moved to her side as they walked toward H.Q., where they'd have to write up an after-action report on their mission.

"Is everything all right, Angel?" He purposely used her first name. Watching her profile, he saw her lips part for a moment at his huskily spoken question. They were crossing the wide flat area and had to watch for zooming golf carts, the main means of transport around the facility.

"Uh, yeah…" Angel frowned. She needed Burke's closeness, even though he left a good foot-and-a-half distance between them as they walked together. "No…" Slowing down, she looked around to make sure they weren't in the way of any golf carts. Looking up into Burke's face, which was cast in shadows by the sulfur lights fixed high above on the cavern ceiling, she saw his gray eyes were wide and searching. Compressing her lips, she whispered, "Look, I'm a little out of sorts…."

"Ever since you laid hands on that old woman who was dying?"

Shrugging, she said, "Yes and no. There's more to the story than you realize, Burke…." Somehow, his name had slipped out again. It felt right to use it. Angel saw his expression melt with relief when she did. Reaching out with her right hand, she briefly touched his arm. "Come on. I need some quiet space. Follow me…." And she moved ahead, toward the lip of the cave, once more.

Without another word, Burke followed as Angel strode quickly toward the cave entrance. The sky outside was dark now, the Eye blocked with dense fog. The yellowish sulfur lights made the ever-moving clouds appear surreal, almost as if he and

Angel were in another world. Maybe they were. He sure felt like it right now. And what he'd seen Angel do today was otherworldly to him, he thought as he watched her move out into the fog and turn a corner.

Staying close on her heels in the dimming light, Burke saw a smaller cave, about seven feet high and five feet wide, in the lava wall. He spotted a few flat stones at the rear. Angel sat down on one of them, her elbows planted on her thighs as she looked up at him.

"Come and sit. We call this our quiet room. It's a small cave that was formed the last time the volcano blew. All the women come here if they want some quiet time or—" her mouth quirked "—to cry, or to spill their guts to their best friend."

"Nice place," Burke offered as he carefully sat his bulk down on a flat, black stone. Because the cave was so small, his left arm was almost touching Angel's right one. Did she mind such close proximity? he wondered. The darkness here was almost complete, except for the fog outside reflecting light from the main cave into this one.

"Yeah, we call this our sanity room." Angel chuckled darkly, then sighed and sat quietly for a long time.

"Listen," Burke said finally, "if this is a private

moment, Angel, I can leave you alone.'' He didn't want to, but he had to make that offer.

"No, it's fine." And it was, to her surprise. So what was different? Angel wasn't sure. Maybe it was the look of compassion she had seen on Burke's face as she'd leaned over the old woman and performed a hands-on healing.

"What's botherin' you then?" Burke asked.

"It's written all over me, huh?"

"I see it. I don't know that everyone sees it."

"You have a highly irritating skill of seeing right through me."

Smiling a little, he cut a glance to his left. Angel's face was shrouded in dimness, but he could see her expression was very sad and pensive. "Somehow, I feel there's an invisible telephone wire strung between us. It's just there, Angel. I didn't manufacture it. It seems to have been there since the day I met you."

"Yeah...I know...."

"It could be worse."

"Oh? Tell me how?"

"I could dislike you."

Her heart pounded briefly. "I haven't been very nice to you since you've come. I've been prickly, like a cactus."

"I figured you had your reasons."

Snorting softly, Angel muttered, "You're a lot more mature than I am. I'm not exactly proud of myself and how I've treated you. It wasn't your fault."

"What wasn't?" Burke knew he was stepping on thin ice with Angel, but he was burning with curiosity about her, about her past. She was mesmerizing to him in so many ways. Mysterious. Exotic.

"I might as well come clean with you," she grumbled. Sitting up, she pushed her hair away from her face. Looking over at Burke, she said, "Five years ago I fell in love with a Peruvian doctor. Sounds great on paper, but the problem was, he was in the army with me. I was enlisted. He was an officer. The two don't mix. It's against regulations for us to fraternize. I was working with him daily, as a paramedic in the field. We'd fly into hot spots where our soldiers were interdicting drug shipments, where bullets were flyin', and we'd be the medical help. Maybe..." she shrugged "...maybe the fear of dying, of being shot at any moment, forged a bond between us, I dunno.... Anyway, Raoul and I fell in love. We didn't mean to—it just happened over time. We knew we shouldn't let it. For a year after that, we very carefully hid our love for one another from everyone else. We'd meet off base, between flights, or we'd take off for Cuzco or some other place where we wouldn't be seen by anyone we knew.''

Burke saw the grief etched in her wide, lustrous eyes as she searched his face. ''You really loved this guy. I can see that,'' he murmured.

Biting her lower lip, Angel whispered, ''Yeah… it's the most painful thing I've ever had happen to me.''

''Did you get found out by military authorities?''

Nodding, Angel quirked her mouth. ''Yeah. We were up at Cuzco, sitting on a bench at Plaza des Armas, when Raoul's commanding officer and his wife just happened by. They were on leave and we didn't know it. All hell broke loose after we got back to Lima, to the army barracks. His C.O. told him to drop me like a hot potato or else. And I got chewed out by my sergeant-major and told the same thing.''

''Tough decision,'' Burke murmured sympathetically. He saw the tears glimmering in her eyes. Though he wanted to put his arm around her shoulders to somehow relieve her pain, Burke fought the desire.

''It was the hardest decision I've ever made. I mean, there I was, one of the few Quero people in the Peruvian army. The Quero are looked down upon, as minorities are in your country. I was a role model. I didn't want the army to think all Queros were no good, or that they were only capable of being farmers. Yes, many of us are farmers, and our ties to the land are strong. The Spanish think we're stupid, so I couldn't blow my career and prove them right. Too many people were watching me and weighing and measuring *all* Queros by my actions." Rubbing her face, Angel muttered, "So, we decided to split up."

"There were other choices you could have made. You could have gotten out. Or he could have decommissioned himself and left the army."

Nodding, Angel said, "Yeah, all the above, except that neither of us wanted to do that, either. We were caught between a rock and a hard place. I wasn't going to end my four-year enlistment, because I was just about the only Quero in the army at that time. The only Quero woman, for sure. I owed it to my people. I wanted them to be proud of me. And I wanted to show those prejudiced bastards that their racist opinion of Queros was dead wrong."

"And Raoul?" Burke saw Angel take angry swipes at her eyes.

"His father was the minister of finance. Raoul was the firstborn son. There was no way he was going to disappoint his family. Besides, when his father found out he was in love with a Quero woman, well, all hell broke loose on that, too. As I said, Spanish Peruvians look down on us. Raoul was in love with a woman below his station.'' Whispering in a painful tone, she continued, "So we called it off. At that time, word came out about a U.S. Army black ops forming near Agua Caliente. They were wanting Peruvian army women as part of that effort. I volunteered. They needed a medical person, and Captain Maya Stevenson took me immediately.''

"So, you put some distance and time between you and Raoul," Burke murmured.

Rubbing her breast above her heart, Angel muttered, "Yeah, something like that.''

"So, are you over him?"

"Yeah…''

"Is that what you meant about an 'honest man'?'' Burke gave her a gentle smile as he searched her shadowed features. Even now he could see the glitter of tears in her eyes.

"It was. Raoul didn't have the guts to come clean about his decision. It really pissed me off. I could have handled the truth—that his father was pressuring him to call off our relationship—but

Raoul lied to me. I lost a lot of respect for him on that one. At least I was honest. But he couldn't be.''

''Then,'' Burke said, ''maybe it was a good thing in disguise.'' Opening his hands, he added wryly, ''Not that I know a lot about relationships, but if a partner can't be honest with you, that's a bad sign.''

''Tell me about it, Tonto.''

Chuckling, Burke added, ''I'm not saying I have all the answers, believe me. My past with women isn't exactly stellar. And the one I got tangled up with…well, let's just say that she was less than honest with me, too.''

Gazing at him, Angel saw a flat look in his shadowed eyes. ''You too? Is it a disease goin' around or what?''

Burke crooked one corner of his mouth. He wanted to tell Angel everything. He didn't know why, he just knew he wanted to open up to her. ''Mary Jo Steele was a secretary who worked for my company commander. I was twenty-three at the time, and fell head over heels for her. She was like a rare, beautiful bird, standing out against the green army drab.''

''A civilian?'' Angel asked curiously. A warmth enveloped her and she found herself wanting to move closer to Burke as he sat there with a pained look on his face.

"Yeah, she was. Pretty, single and bright."

"Well, at least you didn't just fall in love with her body."

Laughing shortly, Burke slanted her a glance. "That counts, but what's in a woman's head counts more. At least with me it does."

"That's good to know. So, you fell for her. What happened?"

"I come from a family with old-fashioned values," Burke told her. "We believe in courting the woman we love. I courted Mary Jo for a year. I guess she found that pretty exciting. At the end of the year, I gave her an engagement ring and she said yes, she'd marry me."

"You got lot farther down the road than I did."

"In some ways, maybe," he murmured quietly.

"So what happened?"

"I didn't know it, but she was having an affair on the side with this captain, an Army Ranger."

"Oww, that hurts. And you didn't suspect?"

Shaking his head, Burke gave her a rueful look. "Blind, deaf and dumb, I suppose."

"But...you loved her and you trusted her. When you love someone, you don't go around asking yourself if she's having an affair behind your back."

"Right on."

Reaching out, Angel placed her hand on his arm. "Dude, we are two of the same kind. Done in by our trust in our partner, whether they deserved it or not."

Her touch was light, nurturing, and Burke found himself yearning deeply for more. Without thinking, he placed his large, hairy hand over her small one. "You didn't deserve that, Angel. You're a good person, with your heart in the right place. I saw that today."

His hand was warm and strong. Caring. Heart pumping in her breast, Angel found herself wanting to simply lean against his firm, broad shoulder. But she didn't dare. She didn't want to fall for this guy. Burke was here on temporary duty; in five weeks he'd walk out of her life forever. So why was her silly heart crying out for him? For his care?

Removing her hand, she sighed and straightened up. "Thanks. But as Maya says, bad things happen to good people all the time." She searched his smoldering gray eyes, which were narrowed upon her. "Look at you. You did everything right by Mary Jo and she screwed you. Royally. And in the worst kind of way." Shaking her head, Angel whispered, "The last four years, I've really questioned myself about relationships. Why do so many fail? Why do so few work? I mean, what *is* it with us two-leggeds? Are we doomed to do nothing but screw up one friendship after another? Never finding real happiness?''

''All questions I've asked myself time and again,'' Burke assured her sardonically.

They both stared out into the darkness, silent for a few minutes. Wispy clouds floated in and out of the cave entrance, as if the earth were breathing with invisible lungs.

Burke looked at Angel. ''Today, out there, something happened.''

She glanced back. ''When?''

''With that old woman, Maria. You laid your hand on her and she instantly relaxed, fell into a deep sleep. And if I wasn't mistaken, I think I saw her smiling a little as she slept.''

''Oh...that...'' Angel shifted uncomfortably.

Scowling, Burke decided to hell with it. He was going to come clean with Angel even if she laughed at him. ''I thought I saw something around you. I was squatting at Maria's' feet, and I know the light in the hut wasn't good, but when you knelt at her side and leaned over her, placing your hand on her chest, I thought I saw something.''

Giving him a narrow-eyed look, Angel said, ''What did you see?''

''Maybe I'm crazy,'' Burke said, shrugging.

"Maybe just stressed out or something, but I saw this gray, cottony cloud surround you." He raised his hand above her head to illustrate. "It started here, above you, and it came down over your upper body. Sort of like a dark gray glove fitting around you."

She stared at him, frowning.

"Was I seeing things? Or was it something more? That old woman was in a lot of pain when we came in. You could see it in her face, the way she was holding herself. And her breathing was labored. As soon as you put your hand on her and this, well…cloud…came over you, she began to relax. Her breathing evened out and she wasn't sucking so hard for air. And then she fell asleep…."

"Didn't you come down here on a fact-finding mission to learn what we do?"

"Yeah," he said, self-deprecating humor in his tone. "And I didn't really know what I was asking."

"In your religion, is there laying on of hands?"

"Sure."

"There is in mine, too."

"So, that's what you did? Laid your hand on her, and then what?"

"I prayed to my spirit guide to send energy from the Inca to the woman, if appropriate."

"Who's the Inca?"

"In our belief system, the Inca is the emperor of the Inca Empire. His wife is known as the Empress." Angel waved her hand toward the mist shifting slowly at the entrance of the cave. "They exist in other dimensions, not this one. They would be akin to what others call God, Buddha, Mohammed or any other great religious deity."

"I see. And something happened after you asked for help for the old lady?"

"Yeah, it did." Shrugging, Angel said, "My parents are medicine people, Burke. I guess I was a chip off the old block, but I never went into training to learn the old ways of our people. Instead, I went off to Cuzco, fought and clawed my way up out of poverty—and made enough money by working three jobs—to go to college. I loved medicine and wanted to be a paramedic."

Impressed, he gave her a slight smile. "You're a scrapper, Angel. You don't take the word *no* lying down, don't just accept someone else's opinion of you. That's a good trait to have."

Hearing the admiration in his voice, Angel felt heat move up her neck and into her face. She was blushing at his compliment. "Thanks…"

"So you became a paramedic?"

"Yeah, and I joined the army. I had a real chip

on my shoulder to prove to the Spanish that any Quero was just as good, if not better, than any one of them.'' She gave him a savage smile. ''I was doing good on that premise until I fell for Raoul.''

''Did this laying on of hands come to you naturally?''

''I was raised with it, Burke. The Quero are a poor but happy people. We recognize our tie with Mother Earth, with the Inca and Empress. Quero medicine people are priests and priestesses to them. I was never officially trained because I was such a wild hellion, growing up in a family of ten kids. I was oldest, and really headstrong. I still am.'' She gave a little laugh. ''I always want to prove to everyone that women are just as good as any man. That Queros are equal to any other nationality, bar none. And even though, as the eldest child I had the right to be trained, I turned the chance down.'' She looked at her right hand, studying it in the dim light. Her nails were blunt cut, her fingers small and slender.

''You have the courage of your convictions,'' Burke said. ''That's your fuel.''

''I guess so.'' Angel looked down at her boots, which had beads of moisture gathering on them. ''To answer your question, Burke, my laying on of hands is something I just automatically do. I *like* to touch people. I like to try and ease their pain in any way I can.''

''That old lady was in a lot of pain today.''

''Yeah.'' Swallowing hard, Angel closed her eyes. When she opened them, she rasped, ''What you don't know is that she's the jaguar priestess for that village. Maria is close to ninety years old. She had been the medicine woman in Yanatin for as long as anyone can recall. Talk about a legend....'' Angel snorted. ''She was a real healer, Burke. She wasn't trained in Western medicine like you or me, but had other abilities—knowledge she used for nearly seventy years in that village before she fell ill.''

''She used her hands, too?'' Burke asked, seeing Angel's face become streaked with falling tears.

''Oh, yeah, she did. She was trained by the Jaguar Clan. It's a mystical and secret clan here in South America. People who want to train for energy work are invited to go to the Village of the Clouds.'' She waved her hand in a northerly direction.

''What do they learn there?''

''About energy. How to use it. How to send it to another person.''

Stumped, Burke sat there trying to understand. ''Energy?''

"Yeah, we're all composed of energy, Burke. But most of us vibrate at a very low frequency." Angel waved her hand at the wisps of fog. "This mist is moving at a higher frequency because it's not as thick and solid as a human being's body is. Essentially, everything is composed of energy and vibration."

"Is this part of your belief system? Or is this quantum mechanics?" He said it partly in jest, because he couldn't stand to see Angel crying. Every part of him, as a man, wanted to comfort her by taking her into his arms. He could tell that Angel needed to have a good long cry. Burke was more than willing to offer the haven of his arms to help her do just that. It had been a long time since he'd been interested in a woman. Angel was like a magical, beautiful bird come into his life, glowing with an inner light that drew him powerfully to her.

Chuckling, Angel wiped her tears away. "Quantum physics is finally catching up to what we know. There was a very famous scientist who came down here a couple of years ago and lived with some Quero shamans in northern Peru. They taught him their secrets. He went back to his country and wrote a book on it. He helped to explain the connection between physics and metaphysics."

"Do you know the name of the book?"

"Sure. I'll write it down for you and you can read it when you go back stateside."

Right now, Burke didn't even want to think of leaving here—or leaving Angel. The last three days might have been miserable, but they'd just had an unexpected breakthrough, and he found himself, like a voracious wolf, hungering for whatever she would share of herself. His past experience with women wasn't good. Since Mary Jo, he had kept most women at arm's length. Oh, he might enjoy them, but he never gave his heart away. Burke couldn't. The damage done to him when he'd been twenty-three still weighed like a warning in his consciousness. And yet Angel was dissolving that old wound by simply being her effervescent self. How was he going to protect himself against her?

Burke wasn't sure he wanted to, though an inner voice warned him strongly that he'd better or he could suffer again. Was the joy of discovery worth the painful price? He wasn't sure. Not yet. Despite the longing in his heart.

Chapter Six

"Hey, Burke, you ready to roll?" Angel stuck her head into the dispensary, where he was helping Elizabeth store some supplies that had just come in. Where had the last two weeks gone? She thought as she saw him lift his head. He was in a red polo shirt and stonewashed jeans that outlined his long, strong legs. There was nothing to dislike about him, she decided. He was in top shape in every sense of the word.

Elizabeth smiled. "Hey, Angel. How you doing?"

Coming into the dispensary, she said, "Better

every day, Doc.'' The caring smile on Liz's full mouth, and the warmth in her eyes, made Angel feel even better. Her left arm was now out of the sling and she showed off her range of movement, which was about forty percent.

"That's great. A little improvement every day." Elizabeth shook her finger in warning as Angel approached her desk. "Now, I know you're going back to Yanatin because there's been an outbreak of an upper respiratory virus there. It's probably flu but don't overdo it, okay? Let Sergeant Gifford help you."

Trying to look humble and acquiescent and not succeeding, Angel murmured, "Of course I will, Doc. I'm learning how to be a woman of leisure, letting a man do all the work for me."

Burke finished lifting the last two cardboard boxes onto chairs in a corner of the office. He turned and grinned at them. "Why do I not believe you, Sergeant Paredes?"

Chuckling, Angel shrugged. "Beats me. You ready, Gifford? The Blackhawk is warming up. Snow Queen's antsy. She wants to get goin'."

Dusting off his hands, he nodded. "Yeah, let's rock 'n' roll." Turning to the doctor, he said, "Is there anything else I can do for you, ma'am?" Today Elizabeth had her shoulder-length red hair in a

French roll, with spiky bangs dusting her forehead. Burke thought she was an exceedingly good-looking woman, and wondered why she wasn't married. She had all the qualities, he felt, that most men would give their right arm for.

Waving her hand, Elizabeth said, "When you get back, Sergeant. Thanks for your help this morning. Now take off, you two."

Once at the village of Yanatin, Angel went straight to the head man's house. Burke walked at her side. In the distance, they heard the Blackhawk disappearing into the clouds. The morning was humid as always, with intermittent rain. As they entered the village on the well-trodden dirt path, Burke frowned. "Looks pretty quiet to me," he noted.

"Yeah," she muttered worriedly. "When Pedro, the head man, sent his son Juan to tell us about the outbreak, I knew it wouldn't be good."

Burke tried not to look too long at Angel. Dressed in civilian clothes she wore a lavender tank top beneath her jacket, and her jeans showed off her shapely legs. Her hair was ruffled from the rotor wash of the Blackhawk. Since the intimate talk they'd shared in the small cave two weeks before, their relationship had changed dramatically. No longer was she irritated by his presence. In fact, an unspoken truce of sorts had developed between them, and he'd breathed an inner sigh of relief.

When they arrived at the plaza, a hard-packed dirt area bordered by many homes, they saw a thatched hut at the center and a number of women hovering over cooking pots out front. Burke noticed there were a lot less children running around playing this time. And though some dogs were hanging around the pots, even they seemed listless. The feeling in the village was subdued, almost depressed, compared with the vibrancy of their earlier visit.

"The problem with flu coming through here," Angel told him as she quickened her pace, "is that these people are now battling white man's diseases. They don't have their immunity built up, so it can worsen and settle in their lungs and might be more devastating than it would be if you or I contracted the same virus."

"If it is a virus," Burke said.

"Yeah, I'm crossing my fingers it's bacterial. If so, we have antibiotics to fight it. If it's a virus, we don't have anything to combat it with."

"We have viral drugs."

"Not here," Angel growled. "They're too expensive for the BJS budget. Liz carries a small amount in the pharmacy, but only for squadron personnel. We can't buy them for the world around us even if we wanted to.''

Nodding, Burke followed her to the hut. Angel knocked on the doorjamb and then slipped past the dark green blanket that was hung over the entrance. Inside, the light was dim. Off to the right, in another room, he saw the old chief. His son Juan greeted them with obvious relief, though anxiety was still written on his face.

Burke heard Angel talk to him in Quechua as they moved into the smaller, cooler room. Fabric was drawn over the window, but that didn't stop the chill of the morning from stealing in. The old chief, Pedro, sat cross-legged on a pallet, coughing violently, his hands across his mouth. His wife, Juana, had a worried look on her face as she knelt next to him, patting his back gently.

Burke went to work. He set down the medical pack and opened it. Pulling out two pairs of latex gloves, for himself and Angel, he quickly tugged his on and knelt on the other side of the old chief. The man's coughing was nonstop, a condition known as rales. Burke scowled as he handed Angel her stethoscope. Grabbing the blood pressure cuff, he got up and moved behind her to wrap it around the old man's left arm.

Angel's eyes narrowed in concentration as she

moved the stethoscope about on his back, listening. Then she got up and moved around him, listening to the front of his sunken chest.

Burke nodded a greeting to Pedro, who had finally stopped coughing, though he was clearly weakened from his illness. Angel got up, retrieved a thermometer and popped it into his mouth. She found a swab and gently slipped it into his nostril then put it in an awaiting vial and capped it. Setting the sample bound for the lab into the pack, she said to Burke, "When we get back, we'll run this through a lab test and see what we're dealing with."

Within ten minutes, they'd taken the old chief's case via examination. Angel got up, gesturing for Burke to follow her out of the hut. Carrying the pack, he walked beside her through the main plaza.

"This is no ordinary flu or upper respiratory infection," she told him. "Juana said Pedro started having a lot of expectoration coming up from his lungs the day we left. He hadn't been feeling well for about a week before that, but no specific symptoms had set in at that time. She said he had a lot of sneezing fits, his eyes would water and he lost his appetite. He barely ate anything the first seven days, and suffered from nighttime coughing, which left her awake, too. Now," Angel continued with a sigh, as she looked back at the hut, "he seems to have gone into a second stage with whatever this is. He's got copious amounts of mucus coming up. You saw it."

"Yeah, there's a lot. I'm worried about possible pneumonia."

"So am I. But...something's not making sense here, Burke, and I can't put my finger on it. At least not yet."

"The old gent is coughing nonstop. His whole body shakes when he gets on a roll," Burke said worriedly.

Rubbing her face, she muttered, "That sound— the coughing sound. I've never heard it before. Have you?"

"No. It's different from normal coughing, that's for sure."

"Maybe we oughta get Liz out here...."

"Let's see if anyone else has these same symptoms first? Then we can take a number of nasal swabs back to the squadron and see, maybe, what we're dealing with?"

"Yeah...good idea." Angel looked up at him and smiled. "You're nice to work with, Burke."

"Good grief, a compliment!"

"Oh, don't let it go to your head, jock."

Chuckling, he reached out and lightly brushed

her cheek. It was the first time he'd ever done something so intimate. Seeing Angel's eyes widen momentarily at his boldness, he leaned over and whispered, "And I like working with you, too. You have a great bedside manner with your patients."

Rattled by his touch, her cheek tingling pleasantly where he'd stroked it, Angel muttered, "Put in a call on the radio to Liz about the swabs coming in, will you? And then contact H.Q. and tell them to send the Blackhawk back here in about an hour."

Taking the radio out of its leather case on his left hip, Burke nodded. He liked the warmth in Angel's dark eyes. She obviously liked his touch. "Okay, you got it."

"This isn't good," Elizabeth murmured. Two days earlier they'd placed the nasal swabs in petri dishes to grow diagnostic cultures. Now as the doctor stood with Angel and Burke in the dispensary, her face was grim. "From what I can see, you're dealing with whooping cough, Angel, not the upper respiratory infection we originally thought."

"Whooping cough?" Angel's voice went high with alarm.

"Damn," Burke whispered, "that's a highly communicable disease."

"No kidding," Angel said, her voice an anxious

whisper. She looked at Elizabeth, who was still frowning down at the lab results. "What can we do, Doc?"

"Whooping cough is not known down here among the Indians," she murmured. "That means they don't have the immune system to combat it. It could race through that village."

"The elderly and the kids are most at risk," Angel said, shaking her head. "If they contract the disease, they'll have problems breathing because of the mucus in their lungs. They may need hospitalization, and we have no way to give them that. What's the drug of choice, Doc?"

"First, we need to vaccinate everyone in the village." Turning, Elizabeth checked her list of vaccines on hand. "I've got whooping cough, but only fifty vials, not enough for a village of two hundred people." Chewing on her lower lip, she said, "I can call the hospital in Cuzco and talk to the doctors there. I'm sure they have the vaccine on hand, and we can have it flown out here to us."

"Okay," Angel said, feeling a cold fear move through her. "We were exposed to it, too, by the way. We had latex gloves on, Doc, but no masks."

"You're up-to-date on your vaccinations," Elizabeth said. "So you two should be spared."

"But what about here?" Burke asked, waving

his hand toward the cave complex. "We could have been spreading it here, too, without realizing it."

"Angel, you need to get into the computer and make sure that everyone is current on their whooping cough vaccination. If they aren't, then we need to get them in here pronto. Okay?"

Angel was already moving to her desk, which stood opposite the doctor's. Sitting down at her computer terminal, she said, "Right on. I'll know in a minute...."

"Have you had outbreaks like this around here before?" Burke asked.

"No," Elizabeth said worriedly. "Whooping cough is new. It's going to be deadly, too. Darn it…this is when I wish we had more medical personnel down here, more medicine...." She turned and went to the locked pharmacy cabinet. Opening it with a small key that hung on a chain around her neck, she took several small boxes and set them on her desk.

"Erythromycin is the antibiotic most recommended for whooping cough. I've got this much on hand. It's not enough."

"Can you get enough from Cuzco? Will they release it to you?" Burke saw there weren't many bottles on her desk.

"Yeah, if I show up with the money," Elizabeth

muttered. Shaking her head, she said, "I've got to see Maya about this. We're in over our heads on this one. We've got an infectious outbreak of a deadly disease and we aren't in a position to stop it. But if we don't get aggressive medical measures into Yanatin, then the whooping cough will spread to other villages, and we could have a wholesale slaughter on our hands. No, I gotta talk to her right away. We need to enlist the help of the Peruvian government on this, as well as hospitals in Cuzco and Lima, to lend support. I'll be back in a little while. Just hang loose."

Burke moved behind Angel as she rapidly checked the vaccination records on all the BJS personnel. "Helluva thing, isn't it?"

"Yeah. You know, that cough…now we both know what it is—whooping cough. I couldn't place it."

"How could you? Since when has either of us ever encountered it? In the U.S.A., everyone's inoculated against it. Down here, they're sitting ducks. We would have never been able to identify it. That's why we were stumped."

Nodding, Angel looked up at him as he stood there, hands in the pockets of his cammies, his dark green T-shirt outlining his broad chest. "I'm still kicking myself. I *knew* something was different. I shoulda thought of it.''

Reaching out, Burke settled his hand on her right shoulder. "Don't be hard on yourself, Angel. You can't fix everything.''

His hand was light and gentle on her shoulder. Absorbing his touch, Angel met his warm gray eyes, which glimmered with feeling—more than she dared accept. The urgency of the outbreak, combined with her need to confide in someone who would understand, took over. "I feel so guilty, Burke. Why didn't I pay more attention to Pedro two weeks ago? Juana said then he wasn't feeling good. Why didn't I take the time to sit down with him and ask about his symptoms?''

"Because,'' he murmured, squeezing her shoulder gently, "you were a little busy with all the other people who were showing serious symptoms, patients who needed your immediate attention, that's why. We aren't mind readers, Angel. Don't beat yourself up over this, okay?''

When Burke took his hand away, Angel felt bereft. How she looked forward to these small, brief touches that somehow seemed to occur naturally between them of late. Every day she fought her feelings for Burke. And every day she found more things to like about him. He was a hard worker.

Responsible. Reliable. All the things she'd once dreamed of finding in a man. And he seemed to be brutally honest at every turn—something Raoul hadn't been. Longing for more personal time with Burke, and knowing she wouldn't be able to get it, Angel felt frustrated and scared. Her heart urged her to reach out to him on a personal level, but her wary head warned her away from such a foolish desire.

"Yeah…but still," she muttered defiantly, shutting off the computer, "if I had known then, we could have moved aggressively on it and not allowed the outbreak to reach this stage." She searched Burke's open face. "We've got twenty-five people with whooping cough in that village. And it's at the infectious stage. Coughing is what spreads it from one person to another.…"

Burke saw tears well up Angel's eyes. Coming around so that he sat on the edge of her desk, he framed her face with his hands and leaned close to her. "Listen to me, will you? We do what we can do and that's it. We're not perfect, sweetheart. We're painfully human. We aren't always going to spot an infectious disease in its beginning stages. You thought he had a cold. So did I."

Closing her eyes, Angel relaxed within his gentle grip. Burke was so close, mere inches away. Gulping in a huge breath of air, she felt the heat of tears gathering behind her closed lids. Opening her eyes, Angel pulled back, away from him. Fear ate at her. She saw Burke straighten and then stand up. As he moved to the other side of the desk, he gave her a dark, searching look.

"Sorry," he murmured. "I don't know what happened...."

Sniffing, Angel swiped at her eyes. He'd called her sweetheart. The endearment riffled through her, like warm sunshine on a cool morning. Now he stood before her looking apologetic, his hands jammed in his pockets, his thick brows knitted.

"We're just upset," Angel managed to answer, trying to shake off the warm feelings his intimacy had evoked within her. "We care. I mean, we're not paramedics for nothing. We *want* to help people. It's our nature." She gave him a sad look.

His mouth curved faintly.

"Yeah, and I found myself wanting to help you, too," he whispered, self-deprecation in his tone.

Feeling awkward, Angel whispered, "It was nice, Burke. I liked it. But it scared the hell outta me, too. *You* scare me."

Giving her a sideways glance, he studied her in the pregnant silence. "Yeah, I scared myself, too."

Laughing a little, Angel said, "Two scared people with bad track records as far as relationships go.

The odds don't look good. Besides, in another month, your TDY is up. You'll be gone.''

"I hear you, Angel. My head knows that." His mouth twisted. "I guess my heart doesn't, though."

Hands clasped in her lap, Angel couldn't meet his searching look. "And I always told myself that honesty was the best policy." She managed a snort and then forced herself to look up and meet Burke's gray eyes.

"Sometimes fear overrides honesty."

"Yeah, that's what it's doing to me right now." Angel rubbed her face. "I'm runnin' scared."

"From?"

"You."

Burke saw her fighting to be honest no matter the cost to her. "Me, too."

"Really?"

He gave her a faint, sad smile. "Yeah. I'm attracted to you, Angel. I was from the start. The last two weeks I've been fighting it, but as you can see, it isn't working...."

"Uh, no, it isn't." Looking around her messy desk, she frowned. "It takes two to tango. I haven't exactly been giving you signals that I didn't like your touches, your attention...."

"I know. Neither of us is blind, deaf or dumb to the other."

Sitting back in her creaky office chair, Angel looked at him. He stood with his head bowed, a serious look on his face, his eyes hooded and unreadable. "Maybe we need to come clean with one another?"

"I've been trying to," he muttered. "After Mary Jo scuttled me…and the love I had for her…I've been running shy of any serious commitments." Lifting his head, Burke stared at Angel. "Until you crashed into my life."

"You're the one who wanted to come down here. I didn't invite you, Gifford."

"That's true, you didn't." He chuckled slightly. "Every day, Angel, I find more and more to admire about you. To like about you. I find your honesty refreshing. You don't play games, and that's important to me."

"Play games? Not a chance," Angel said. "I'm just so scared, Burke. You're temporary down here. I find myself wanting to know you better. Much better. At any given hour, I'm either scared to death or I feel like I'm flying high."

"Yeah. Me, too."

"Great."

"Well," he said, holding her warm gaze, "it's up to us to decide how we want to handle this…

what's happening to us. Whether we want it to or not.''

"I know," Angel whispered. "I never thought of myself as a coward. But I am, Burke. I'm scared of getting into a real relationship. Oh, it's one thing to go dancin' in Cuzco with guys. It's totally another to think about…well, long term.''

"I see the hurdles, too," he agreed. "I have a career to think about, as you do. I'm in the job of my dreams at the base as a teacher-paramedic. And you love what you do down here. You're making a difference, and that is just as rewarding.''

"It is," Angel agreed quietly. She laced her fingers across her belly and rocked back in her chair. "I wish you could have been like those Neanderthal army dawgs who think women are second-class citizens.''

"And I wish you could have been a woman who was coy and manipulative.''

"Well, at least neither one of us acts badly as a result of our past experience with our partners?''

Shaking his head, Burke murmured, "True.''

"You know, one of our Apache pilots is married to Jake. She's Peruvian and Jake is *norteamericano*. He used to be in the army until he resigned his commission to come down here to look for his sister, who had been kidnapped by a local drug lord.

Jake and Ana live here now, over in housing on the mining side of the mountain. Ana still flies. Jake is the head of our agricultural efforts, and he also takes care of Supply. I see how happy they are, Burke. They really love one another. I always thought all relationships would sour, but theirs has taken off and they soar like condors—together.''

"Yeah, I've met both of them at different times. The other night, when you were over here logging in supplies, I was at the mess hut and sat down and ate dinner with them. They seem happy.''

"I've been analyzing them,'' Angel said. "I watch them. I listen to how they talk with one another. I compare it to what I had with Raoul.''

Burke saw her brows knit as she pondered her words. "Big differences?''

"Yeah, striking. Glaring. Ana and Jake are open and honest with each other. The thing they have in common is their respect for one another. I've seen them disagree, but they talk it out like adults. Neither one sinks to childish or immature behavior. And they *like* one another, Burke. They're the best of friends. Jake loves his gardens, and you can find Ana down there with him, on her hands and knees, muddy from head to toe from weeding, but happy as a clam. They love sharing what they do.''

"When I look back on Mary Jo, and the games

she was playing, I ask myself why didn't I see it then. I've watched Ana and Jake as you have, and there're no games between them. I guess it comes back to honesty, doesn't it?''

Giving him a jaded look, Angel said, ''Honesty is the best policy.''

''So? Where does that leave us?''

Chapter Seven

Where did that leave them? Angel wondered later, as she sat at a table in the mess hall, a cup of coffee in hand. Though Burke sat opposite in silence, his words still haunted her. She felt as if they were both standing on a precipice and looking down—a long way down. If they stepped off together, they would die. That was how she felt. When she saw how Burke stared down at the cup between his large hands, his brows knitted darkly, she knew he was pondering the same thing.

Lifting his head, he settled his gaze on her. ''We never completed our conversation about

Maria, the jaguar priestess in Yanatin you laid your hands on.''

Almost relieved to discuss anything other than personal feelings, Angel brightened. "This is the heart of your fact-finding mission, you know," she teased.

"Yeah, I guess it is. I've been turning the whole thing around in my mind. Chewin' on it, I guess. I didn't know what I was requesting when I came down here, but that's all right. Fools rush in where angels fear to tread. I've gone through my limited knowledge of other cultures and belief systems, and I can't think of any that don't have hands-on healing as a part of them. Can you?" He searched her fathomless dark gaze. Angel's eyes always reminded him of at the night sky, shining with such life, the sparkle in them reminding him of bright stars. Burke would never tire of looking at her slightly asymmetrical face, that soft mouth usually curved in a faint smile filled with deviltry. Angel liked to laugh. And she was good at teasing repartee, something he enjoyed immensely. Give and take, that's what it was. It was easy to exchange comments, humor and ideas with Angel. Another point in her favor, whether Burke wanted to admit it or not.

"Touching never goes out of style, Burke."

His mouth pulled down slightly. Running his fingers across the white ceramic cup, he nodded. ''Yeah, you're right.''

''That's all it is,'' Angel said. ''Touching another human being with love is healing. That's how I see it. All Quero realize the value of touch.''

''North Americans aren't much into the touching department.''

''That's a pity.''

''Yeah, I think it is.'' He cocked his head and studied her. ''But something *else* happened. I saw it. Or I saw *something*. I'm not sure what. Did you feel different when you touched her?''

Shrugging, Angel said, ''In my culture, healers have spirit guides. Because I never went into training, I don't have a clue as to what or who mine is. All I can guess is that what you saw was my guide.''

''What, exactly, is a guide?''

Sipping her coffee, she murmured, ''Your religion would call them guardian angels, I think. Down here, we work with the natural world around us, so our guides take on the shapes of insects, reptiles and animals that live around us.''

''I see. But as I understand it, guardian angels are there to keep us out of trouble.''

Chuckling, Angel said, ''Well, we have a differ-

ent take on it down here. Our guides are our teachers. We're the students, and the guides try to whisper to us and teach us. Now—'' she straightened
and smiled ''—whether we listen or not is another
question.''

''So,'' Burke said, trying to understand, ''this
gray cloud that came over the upper half of your
body was your guide?''

Shrugging, Angel muttered, ''I don't know. I
wasn't aware of it, Burke.''

''Yet I saw Maria relax when this thing came
over you, surrounded you. Didn't you feel anything?''

Holding up her hands, Angel said, ''My fingers
get red-hot when I place them on a person. But it's
not a physical heat. It's energy pulsing through
them to her—to whomever I'm touching.''

''Does this energy come from you?''

''Better not,'' Angel laughed. ''If it does, then
I'd feel wiped out afterward, for sure. No, my
mother taught me to ground myself and ask for the
energy to come through to help the other person.
All I have to do is put my mind in neutral, think
of nothing, close my eyes and let it flow. In essence,
Burke, I become a conduit tube through which the
energy flows.''

"Well," he muttered, "where does this energy come from? Your guide, then?"

"It can. But it can also come from Mother Earth, too. Don't forget, she's our real mother. We're her children. If we just ask her for healing energy, she'll send it up through our feet and into our body to help us, or to help another."

"Which type was being given to that priestess?"

"Umm." Angel looked up toward the ceiling in thought. "I remember asking my guide for help."

"And then what happened? You said your hands got hot?"

"Well, that day I laid only my right hand on her because my left was in a sling. I grounded myself, I closed my eyes, I stopped my mind from chattering, and then I felt this warmth coming down my arm and into my hand. That's what it usually feels like."

"Okay," Burke murmured, turning the cup slowly around in his hands, "is this something only a few trained people can do?"

Shaking her head, Angel said, "No. Anyone, as far as I know, can do it. All you need is to have your heart in the right place, a desire to help. If you care about someone—even an animal or a plant, let's say—you can do it. Even *you* can, Burke." She grinned. Liking the warmth banked in his gray eyes, Angel felt her heart opening beneath his smoldering inspection. What would it be like to kiss him? To touch him the way a woman touches her man? The thought was intriguing. Scary.

"Me?"

"Sure. We'll be going back to the village in a little while, with supplies, and you can try it. Just ground yourself."

"How do I do that?"

"Close your eyes and see silver tree roots wrapping gently around your ankles, and the tips of the roots moving through the center of each of your feet, then diving a couple hundred feet down into Mother Earth. You never attempt healing without being grounded. If you do, you can take on the symptoms of the person you're trying to help, and then you're going to be very sorry and very miserable afterward. If you do, it usually takes one or two days to get rid of them."

Shaking his head, Burke said, "I don't think I can do what you do."

"Then your belief that you can't will stop you from being successful." Angel tapped her head. "Our reality is here. It's what we want it to be. If I believe that I can be a pipe through which universal loving energy can flow to help another person, it will be so. And if you don't believe you can do it, that will be so, too.''

"Is that how you saved the lives of people who shouldn't have lived?"

Smiling thinly, Angel said hesitantly, "Yes. But let's get this in proper perspective, Burke. I asked for healing energy for that person at the time. I don't have a decision as to whether or not it flows through me to them. I don't control it. All I am is a transfer point, a connection between it and the person."

Sitting there, Burke looked at her. "Okay, another hardball question." He pointed to her left shoulder, which was healing now from the tendon inflammation. Angel had about sixty percent mobility but still couldn't use her arm a lot. Not yet, at least. "Why can't you heal yourself? Put your hand on your left shoulder and ask for help?"

"I did," she laughed. "Nothing happened!"

"Why?"

"Because, whatever this—" she pointed at her left shoulder "—is about, it's mine to work through, and to grasp."

"What do you mean?"

"Anytime we get sick in the physical body, Burke, it's an accumulated result of where we're at with our head and our heart. I know Western medicine doesn't give a damn about this aspect of healing and illness, but I was trained to see it from that perspective.''

''Okay,'' he murmured, ''what does a shoulder symbolize?''

''Heavy loads and burdens. Responsibilities we carry on them. Think about it.''

''You were carrying too heavy a load, so your shoulder 'broke,' so to speak?''

''Now you're getting the idea,'' Angel said.

''Your responsibilities here—'' he looked around the mess, which was pretty much deserted right now ''—are overwhelming?''

''They are,'' Angel said reluctantly. ''My department's understaffed, and we're getting more and more men personnel here at BJS. Elizabeth and I are working twelve, fourteen hours a day, with no time off. It's brutal.''

''So your shoulder became inflamed so you could get some rest?''

''That's pretty much it in a nutshell,'' Angel murmured. ''I needed a rest. I didn't ask for it and I should have. I know how inundated we are and I didn't want to put an extra load on the doc by taking off for a week's leave just to catch up on sleep and kick back.''

''Your body rebelled on you, then?''

Play the Romance Crossword Game

and get...

2 FREE BOOKS

and a

FREE GIFT...

YOURS to KEEP!

Scratch Here!

to reveal the hidden words.
Look below to see what you get.

Yes!

I have scratched off the gold areas. Please send me my **2 FREE BOOKS** and **FREE GIFT** for which I qualify. I understand that I am under no obligation to purchase any books as explained on the back of this card.

DETACH AND MAIL CARD TODAY!

335 SDL DRTS   235 SDL DRT9

FIRST NAME

LAST NAME

ADDRESS

APT.#

CITY

STATE/PROV.

ZIP/POSTAL CODE

Visit us online at
www.eHarlequin.com

ROMANCE	MYSTERY	NOVEL	GIFT
You get **2 FREE BOOKS** PLUS a **FREE GIFT!**	You get **2 FREE BOOKS!**	You get **1 FREE BOOK!**	You get a **FREE MYSTERY GIFT!**

The Silhouette Reader Service™ — Here's how it works:

Accepting your 2 free books and mystery gift places you under no obligation to buy anything. You may keep the books and gift and return the shipping statement marked "cancel." If you do not cancel, about a month later we'll send you 6 additional books and bill you just $3.99 each in the U.S., or $4.74 each in Canada, plus 25¢ shipping & handling per book and applicable taxes if any.* That's the complete price and — compared to cover prices of $4.75 each in the U.S. and $5.75 each in Canada — it's quite a bargain! You may cancel at any time, but if you choose to continue, every month we'll send you 6 more books, which you may either purchase at the discount price or return to us and cancel your subscription.

*Terms and prices subject to change without notice. Sales tax applicable in N.Y. Canadian residents will be charged applicable provincial taxes and GST. Credit or Debit balances in a customer's account(s) may be offset by any other outstanding balance owed by or to the customer

If offer card is missing write to: Silhouette Reader Service, 3010 Walden Ave., P.O. Box 1867, Buffalo, NY 14240-1867

BUSINESS REPLY MAIL
FIRST-CLASS MAIL   PERMIT NO. 717-003   BUFFALO, NY

POSTAGE WILL BE PAID BY ADDRESSEE

SILHOUETTE READER SERVICE
3010 WALDEN AVE
PO BOX 1867
BUFFALO NY 14240-9952

NO POSTAGE
NECESSARY
IF MAILED
IN THE
UNITED STATES

"Yeah, you could say that," Angel said wryly, searching his pensive features as he mulled all this over. Sipping her coffee, she asked, "Did you have any physical symptoms after Mary Jo broke up with you?"

Sitting back, Burke thought about that time. A slow grin spread across his mouth. "Yeah, come to think of it…about two weeks afterward, I had a tooth blow up on me. It abscessed, and I had to get it taken care of."

"See? When we jam any of our unspoken emotions down inside of us, they blow out somewhere. Anytime there's inflammation, that's symbolic of anger. You probably were really angry at her, wanted to say some pretty heated words to her, but you didn't. You clamped down on your rage and swallowed it, but it didn't go away. You didn't open your mouth and speak out, didn't express your anger to her, so your tooth got inflamed instead."

"That's a pretty interesting take on things, Angel."

"It's how I live my life." She touched her left shoulder gingerly. "I was really frustrated. Frustration is anger of another form. I wanted to go home to my village, to visit my parents and see my family once again. Work around here has been so intense and unrelenting that my frustration mounted. My loyalty to the doc, to BJS, overrode my more personal, emotional needs.''

''And if you had gotten some leave and gone home, you don't think your shoulder would have flamed up on you?''

''That's right. Emotionally, I'd have been taking care of me instead. But I'm pretty bullheaded, and my loyalty to BJS took precedence when it shouldn't have. This is the result. We're all responsible for the good and bad choices we make, Burke.'' Angel smiled slightly. ''But it wasn't all bad. You came down here to be my hands and arms. Even bad choices can have some pretty good consequences sometimes.''

''I'm not sorry I came down here, Angel. I'm just trying to figure out how to write all this up in my report to the major, the head of the medical school where I teach.''

''Yeah,'' Angel chortled, ''I'm gonna be real interested in how you explain this to him. *Delicately* is a word I'd use.''

''When you're out in the field with a Special Forces A team, the medic with them isn't looking to lay hands on someone if they get wounded,'' Burke noted with a frown.

''No, but consider this. In my job as a paramedic around here, we've worked with A teams before.

On one mission, we had to pick up the only soldier who survived and a senator's daughter who had been kidnapped by druggies. The soldier's leg was a mangled mess from a brush with a rocket. He was bleeding out on me. I knew that he'd lost a lot of blood and we couldn't replace it fast enough. Once I got him stabilized by traditional medical methods, I put my hands above his knee and asked for energy to flow into him to stop the bleeding.''

"What happened?''

"The hemorrhaging stopped in five minutes. He stabilized and we got him to a Cuzco hospital, where he went into emergency surgery.''

"Does this guy know what you did?''

Shaking her head, she said, "No. And I didn't tell him, either. You can use this method out in the field, Burke. You can train people to do it. It's very easy.''

"Will you train me? When we go back to Yan-atin, and after we've done what we can through traditional medicine, will you show me how to do this?''

Heartened by his sincerity, Angel nodded. "Sure, no problem.''

"Here,'' Angel told Burke as she carried a two-year-old girl over to where he sat in the hut, "training time.'' Placing the little girl, who had the first stage of whooping cough, in his arms, she knelt down in front of him. Hands on her knees, Angel looked up at the concerned parents who watched. She explained quickly in Quechua to them what Burke was going to do. They nodded, hope burning in their eyes.

Burke sat on the hard-packed earthen floor in the family's bedroom. The pallets were all rolled up and tucked neatly along one wall. A sputtering oil lamp provided the only light. They'd worked non-stop for six hours, giving vaccinations and handing out antibiotics to those affected. Angel had gotten permission to remain in the village for the next three days to try and contain the outbreak. Tomorrow morning, the Blackhawk would bring in more desperately needed medical supplies. Angel and Burke had just exhausted the last of what they had with them. All that was left was hands-on healing.

Swaddled in a pink alpaca blanket, the black-haired little girl looked up at him, eyes wide, as he cradled her gently in his arms. He looked to Angel for guidance. She smiled slightly and tucked the blanket around the child's shoulders to make sure she was as warm as possible. The drafts in the hut were chilly at night and the child was sick and extra vulnerable.

"Close your eyes, Burke. Take a couple of deep breaths to help you relax." Angel kept her hands on her thighs as she watched him do as she suggested. Just the way Burke cradled the child made her feel warm inside. He was good with babies and children. Throughout the afternoon hours, as they'd gone from hut to hut administering to the families, he'd been marvously gentle with the sick children. Not every man had this kind of maternal instinct, but Burke did, and it made Angel's heart reel with appreciation.

"Okay, I'm there," he told her, his hands wrapped gently around the quiet child.

"Great. Now, in your forehead, see the silver roots wrapping around your ankles and going down through your feet into Mother Earth."

Nodding after a minute or so, he said, "Okay...that was tough."

"Just imagine it," Angel instructed. "Now ask your guardian angel to send the healing energy through your hands to the baby in your arms. It's that simple. Try not to think while this is happening. Shut off your mind chatter, if possible. Try to stand out of the way. See your arms and hands as empty pipes...."

Burke tried it. Nothing happened. He waited, feeling the pressure of expectation. He could hear the low voices of the parents in the background, whispering to one another, and it broke his concentration.

"Nothing," he said abruptly.

"Be patient," Angel advised. "This is the first time you've tried it. It takes a while to unhinge and open up all those rusty doors inside your head to allow this to happen." She chuckled quietly, then, reaching out, put her hand on his left knee. "Expect nothing, receive everything. That's a good state to put yourself in. Just relax."

Burke struggled to get rid of the expectation. It wasn't easy after seeing the parents' faces burning with hope. He swallowed hard and tried to relax. Angel's hand on his knee made him feel less anxiety. The little girl was quiet in his arms, even though her breathing was noisy and labored.

And then it happened. Burke was so busy worrying that the little tyke was going to get worse in the night because they had no medicine to give her until morning, that at first he wasn't aware of the warming sensation that began to travel from his elbows downward toward his hands. His eyes snapped open. Angel was leaning toward him, her hand still on his knee, watching him with a tender look on her face.

"It's happening!"

"What?"

"The heat. I feel the heat in my arms." Burke wondered if he was imagining it.

Angel grinned broadly. "Cool, dude. Okay, close your eyes, breathe deeply and evenly and just let it flow. Your guardian angel knows where this energy needs to go...."

He sat there for ten minutes, feeling his hands become tingly and warmer than usual. It was cool and damp in the hut, and there was no way to explain away the heat sensation he was feeling. His hearing keyed in on the little girl. If it wasn't his imagination, her breathing was less raspy, the noise in her nose and chest lessening. Burke knew he could verify if that was true. He'd listened to her lungs with his stethoscope beforehand. After this training session, he'd check her lungs again. If this really worked, her breathing should be a lot less labored.

Opening his eyes, he looked at Angel. With the oil lamp behind her, her face was deeply shadowed, her dark hair tousled. There was a warm look in her hooded gaze, and a soft smile lingered on her lips.

"It's gone," he told her. "The warmth, I mean."

"That's fine," she reassured him, taking the girl into her arms and holding her. "Your guardian decided she'd had enough.'' Looking down at the girl, who gazed up at her, Angel said, ''Have you noticed her breathing is easier? Less noisy?''

Reaching for his pack, Burke pulled out his stethoscope. ''Yeah. Open up the blanket and let me listen to her lungs.''

''Sure.'' Angel propped the baby girl against her chest and loosened her blanket so he could use the stethoscope to listen to her lungs.

''I'll be damned!'' Burke breathed softly. Pulling the stethoscope out of his ears, he stared at Angel. She was tucking the blanket back around the baby. The mother came over and took her out of Angel's arms with a murmured thank-you.

''Well?'' Angel asked, grinning. ''Better?''

''Yeah. I can't explain it. Her breathing was bad before. You could hear the crackling sounds in her lungs.''

''And now?''

''Now...'' Burke put the stethoscope back into the canvas bag at his side ''...they're gone.''

''Yep,'' Angel said, getting to her feet and dusting off her pants, ''that's how it works.''

Stymied, Burke slowly unwound and stood up. He was tall compared to the Quero, who averaged five to five and a half feet in height. Both parents stood huddled around their baby girl, giving him grateful looks.

"Come on," Angel said, "I want to visit the old priestess and see how she's doin', and then we can call it a night. They've got an empty hut at the end of the village where we'll stay."

It was nearly 2100, and Burke knew he ought to be dead on his feet, but he wasn't. A short while later, he followed Angel out the blanketed entrance of Maria's hut and back to the plaza, where small cooking fires created enough light to see where they were walking.

"That's amazing," he said, remembering how Maria had smiled in welcome. Angel had simply put her hands on the woman's upper chest, and just as before, her breathing had eased.

"Yeah. What's more amazing is that anyone can do this, Burke." Angel smiled up at him. "I'm really proud of you! You did good that first time out. If you don't have medical supplies you need, you always have your hands, you know?"

Frowning, he said, "Does it hold? This energy, I mean? Maria's dying and I see it giving her temporary relief. Will that little girl be stable?"

Angel nodded. "Yeah, she will be. But you can go back tomorrow morning and check out her lungs and see for yourself. As for Maria, she is in the hands of the Inca. My spirit guide gives her what she needs. In her case, it's her time to die, but that doesn't mean we can't be of assistance.'' Smiling, Angel said, ''Oh, I can hardly wait until your superior reads your report on this.''

Chapter Eight

The two-room hut they'd been given to stay in was near the edge of the village, close to the jungle. In its quiet intimacy, Burke was wildly aware of Angel, in so many ways. It was 2200, 10:00 p.m., and as she spread two pallets side by side in the tiny bedroom, he hesitated in the doorway.

"You don't mind sleeping next to me?" he asked.

Angel smoothed out the thick cotton mats, moving around on her hands and knees. With her left shoulder healing, she could put some weight on her arm, and was developing more mobility. "No.

Why? Do you snore like a freight train? If you do you're going to sleep outside.''

Entering the room, he took a cotton quilt and unfolded it. Angel was giving him that devilish smile again. The room was barely large enough for both of them. There was hardly two feet between the pallets and the walls. "I do snore...."

"So do I," he laughed.

Chuckling, he said, "Everyone does. It's sort of refreshing to hear a woman admit to it."

Sitting on the edge of her pallet, Angel began to unlace her boots. Handing her the quilt, he joined her, and she reveled in his closeness.

"Yeah, that kills me. I mean, everyone has a nose and pharynx." She shook her head. The small oil lamp on the table in the other room sputtered, and the dim light cast shadows across his face as he leaned down to remove his boots.

"Well," he teased, "if I wake you up, swing an elbow into my ribs and make me turn on my side. I snore when I'm on my back."

"Same here," Angel said, placing her boots to one side and crossing her legs.

Sitting there, his hands draped across his knees, Burke watched the shadows caress Angel's strong features. All day he'd wanted to touch her, kiss her. Getting up the courage, he reached out and started to unbutton her jacket. Then, sliding his hand to her left shoulder, carefully so as not to jostle her injury, he whispered, "Time for some honesty on my part..."

Shocked by the unexpected intimacy, Angel looked up into his dark, chiseled face. The look in his narrowed eyes made her heart pound wildly, her mouth go suddenly dry.

"What?" she asked, her voice an off-key whisper.

Holding her hand gently in his, Burke turned so that he was facing her, his legs bracketing hers. She was small compared to his bulk and height, but that took nothing away from her strength as a woman. "I keep asking myself, Angel, why I'm so drawn to you. The more I know of you, the more I want to make our time together count." He quirked his mouth as he saw her eyes grow huge with surprise. "This is probably one-sided. My side. And you have to believe that I didn't come down here with desire for you on my mind. Yeah, I was excited to meet you, to do this fact-finding mission. But what I didn't expect was to...well, be drawn to you like I am."

Blinking, Angel let out a little sigh. She liked the way Burke's strong fingers gently stroked hers. Seeing the unsureness, the fear in his eyes, she licked her lower lip nervously. "I—I see...."

Feeling scared, Burke held her gaze, saw the turmoil there. "Is this one-sided, Angel? Am I the only one feeling this or—"

"No," she said, her voice low and fervent, "it's a two-way street, Burke." Shrugging, she continued, "I've been fighting my attraction to you, too. My head tells me I'm crazy. After Raoul, I swore I'd never be drawn to another man. My heart can't stand rejection like that twice. It just can't."

"I understand...I really do."

"And Mary Jo did you in. We both got nailed in the heart."

"Yeah, but my crazy heart has decided it likes you."

Hanging her head, Angel felt his fingers close more firmly over hers. "Mine, too...."

"We sound like we've been given a death sentence over it."

Her laugh rueful, Angel raised her head and met his stormy eyes. "I'm scared, Burke. Scared as hell."

"Me, too."

"You're going to be gone in a month. You're never comin' back."

"I know...." Burke clearly read the frustration in her face, in the set of her lips.

"I'm not one of these women who loves and leaves, or bed hops. I'm just not built emotionally for it, Burke."

"I know that. That's why I've been fighting my attraction to you."

Angel sat there, eyes closed. The sounds of crickets and frogs in the nearby jungle reached them as she tried to think her way through their predicament. It was easier to talk without looking at him. "Do you know how nice it feels to have you hold my hand like that?" she asked, her voice low and halting. "Since you've been here, I've found myself starved for you in every way possible. I think I tried to fool myself that I didn't need a man in my life, but that's a lie, too."

"We're caught in the same lie, then," Burke admitted quietly. Angel opened her eyes and gazed at him. He studied each of her slender, small fingers—the hands of a healer. Something in him told him that Angel could heal the wound in his heart. But how? In a month he'd be gone. Confused, Burke said nothing.

Nodding, Angel whispered, "You know what I want? What I *really* want?"

''No. Tell me.'' His heart pounded a little at the look of desire burning in her dark eyes.

''I'd like to sleep with you. I mean, be held by you. I'm not ready to make love with you, Burke. That's a step—a commitment—I'm not ready for. But if you could handle it…I'd like to put our two pallets together, snuggle up and just sleep in your arms.''

''I can do that.'' Silence lapsed between them. Finding courage, he asked, ''Do you know what I really want?''

''No. Tell me.''

''I want to kiss you.''

Her lips tingled in anticipation. Without a word, Angel got to her knees, released his hand and moved between his opened legs. Placing her hands on his broad shoulders, she knelt in front of him. ''So do I.…'' And she leaned down, slid her fingers behind his thickly corded neck and drew him forward.

Burke liked her bold assertiveness. Slipping his hands around her back, he leaned upward to meet her lips. In that moment, the natural world around them seemed to break into a melodic symphony. Monkeys screaming in the distance, the croaking frogs and chirping crickets all conspired to create a haunting, fragile atmosphere that embraced them.

As Angel's mouth brushed his, Burke felt her softness and strength simultaneously. Moving his hands upward, he caressed her neck, tunneling his fingers into her thick, silky black hair. Opening his mouth, he brought her more surely against his body. She smelled of smoke from the cooking fires, the heady scent of orchids found in nearly every hut, and that special fragrance that was Angel's alone.

Moaning, Angel capitulated completely as Burke's mouth moved strongly, yet caressingly against hers. His beard was like sandpaper against her cheek, but she didn't care. His breath was ragged against her cheek as she absorbed everything about this man. She felt him holding back, as if for her sake. It was a kiss, nothing more, and yet Angel felt a wild, gnawing ache building deep within her—a yearning to complete herself with Burke. But if she did that, this would be more than just a fleeting, stolen kiss. It would be a commitment. And she knew neither of them was ready to take that step.

His mouth was coaxing, moving hotly, wetly across hers. As his tongue explored her lower lip and his hands ranged across her scalp, she moaned. She found herself starved for Burke. Maybe that was due to five years without a man in her life. Angel wasn't sure. Just having Burke's strong arms around her, pressing her hotly against him while taking care not to crush her injured shoulder, was a heady feeling. One she cherished.

Finally, reluctantly, Angel broke their hungry kiss. Settling back on her heels, her arms resting on his shoulders, she looked up at him. His eyes were silvery with the fire of desire he felt for her. When he lifted his hand and brushed several strands of hair off her brow, she managed a wobbly smile. "Wow," she whispered.

"Yeah."

"I didn't expect…well…"

"Shh, you don't have to say a word, sweetheart. I'm feeling the same thing." Burke gave her a grudging smile. His body was tied in hot, fiery knots. He wanted Angel so badly he ached. And yet he understood the ground rules with her. To force himself on her, to try and take her, would be wrong. Right now, they were building trust with one another. Because they were unsure where their relationship would go, Burke had to be content to simply share a kiss with Angel. Running his hands over her mussed hair, he whispered, "You still want to sleep with me? I'll just hold you, I promise. No funny stuff."

Nodding, Angel whispered, "Yeah…I'd like that a lot, Burke."

* * *

The whapping of helicopter blades woke Angel from her deep sleep in Burke's arms. She lay on her side, facing him, his arms around her. Although clothed, she could still feel the wonderful heat and security of having him against her.

Was she having a nightmare? The helicopter was getting closer and closer. She could feel the vibration of the blades shaking the hut and trembling through her. The chopper was close. Too close. What was going on?

And then Angel heard sharp warning cries from several villagers.

Almost simultaneously, she felt Burke jerk, as if an electrical charge had coursed through him.

Something was wrong.

Eyes barely open, Angel felt Burke leave her side.

"What...?" she mumbled, struggling to sit up.

"Listen!" Burke said as he sat up tensely, his brain spongy as he tried to reorient himself. It was still dark. What time was it? He held up his wrist and looked at the illuminated dials: 0300.

Rubbing her eyes, Angel gasped. The helicopter was real! And it wasn't one of theirs. She could tell by the sound of the engine.

"Oh, damn!" she cried. "Druggies! Burke, we

gotta get outta here! They're comin' in with choppers! They find us here and we're dead! Get up! Get up!''

Still disoriented, Burke got to his feet. They both fumbled for their boots, jamming their feet into them. The oil lamp sputtered nastily on the wooden table in the other room. The hut was shaking like a dog getting rid of fleas.

Angel leaped for the door, grabbing her knapsack off the table. ''Come on, Burke! We gotta make a run for the jungle. If they find us, we're dead! They'll know we're black ops people. We're their enemy! Hurry!''

Within seconds, they'd lunged out the door and headed down one of the many paths into the jungle. Burke hung back a step. They had side arms, 9 mm Berettas, but that was all. He knew they weren't prepared to face an armed drug force landing in a helicopter. The only smart thing to do was fade away into the jungle until the copters left.

Angel's nighttime vision was excellent. Usually, with the jungle's high humidity, a veil of fog hung around the treetops, but not tonight. The full moon cast a silvery radiance through the forest, providing enough light for her to see where she was going. Luckily, she knew the village of Yanatin well, and all the various footpaths that had been hacked into the jungle around it. Behind her, she heard a second helicopter landing.

Burke caught up with her. The path was wide enough for two people to jog shoulder to shoulder.

"Two helos," he panted.

"Yeah. My guess one's a Kamov Black Shark. It sounds like one. If it is, Burke, and someone in the village tells them about us, they're gonna be up and hunting for us. It's got infrared on board. They can spot our body heat anywhere in this jungle."

Nodding, he said, "Where are we going?"

"To a cave at the end of this path. There's a small river about a mile from here—a volcanic area with plenty of small caves to hole up in. We'll be safe from infrared if they decide to hunt us. It can't penetrate a cave."

"Sounds good." Burke looked over his shoulder, worried that they might be followed. Angel picked up the pace as the path swung gently downward. He stayed at her heels, jogging easily. The pack on his back slapped against him, but he was glad he'd taken it along. His medical pack, the large one, had been left behind. Would the druggies search every hut? Would the villagers give away the fact that he and Angel were here? He felt as if he were in over his head, in an unfamiliar combat situation he hadn't been briefed for.

Within ten minutes, they reached their destination. They were both breathing heavily as Angel led him along the bank of the shallow river. To their right was a series of jutting lava cliffs. Burke narrowed his eyes. He could see the patches of darkness indicating caves. Scrambling through the wet, knee-high grass, he followed Angel as she headed to the nearest cave. She dived inside, scrambling toward the rear on her knees, bracing herself with her one good hand. Burke shrugged out of his pack, dropped to his own hands and knees and quickly followed her.

Angel scooted against the back wall, removing the sweat from her face as Burke joined her. The cave was roughly eight feet wide and five feet high, and long like a tunnel. There was no way a Kamov could shoot infrared into it and detect their body heat.

"That was a helluva wake-up call," Burke growled, opening his pack to find a bottle of water. Uncorking it, he handed it to Angel.

"Thanks," she gasped, and drank deeply. Wiping her mouth, she handed the bottle back to him. "Yeah, I sure wasn't expecting druggies to drop in."

"Does it happen often?" Burke asked, drinking

in turn, then capping the bottle and sliding it back in his pack.

"No, not often. But a number of drug lords are tryin' to take over this turf. Yanatin is a large village, situated between the edge of the jungle and the lowlands where coca is grown. The villagers used to be forced into growing it, collecting the leaves and then making it into cocaine, until Major Houston and the Peruvian army came in and started giving them some protection. And when Maya dusted off the head drug lord a year ago, this whole region sort of fell into chaos." Angel tried to steady her breathing. She was scared. Druggies were known to routinely put bullets into the head of anyone who wasn't Quero. She was, of course, but they'd know instantly that she wasn't from Yanatin. And they'd murder Burke in a heartbeat.

Straining his ears, Burke could faintly hear the helicopters in the distance. "So what are they doing? Why did they come in at this time of night?"

"My guess is that some drug lord's trying to scare the villagers by showing up outta the blue."

"What will they do?"

"Probably hassle Pedro, the head man. He's so sick! I feel so sorry for him and his family...." Angel choked up abruptly. Then she felt Burke's hand find hers, squeezing her fingers gently.

"Will they kill him? His family?"

"No. They'll just put the fear of God into him by threatening to do so. They'll go around booting people out of their huts, putting guns to their heads just to scare them. They'll keep the helos up and running to throw more fear into them by all the noise. They'll probably have a transport helo for the drug soldiers and a Kamov along to fly cover and protection for it, as well as provide the fire-power. That's usually how they do it. Maya had worked hard to stop this stuff but we're only one military ops and Peru is a large country."

"Did Pedro say they've been here before?"

Shaking her head, Angel wiped the sweat off her face. "I asked him about that the other day, and he said no one had been bothering them for over a year. No, this is new."

Sitting there, Burke thought out loud. "We have no way to reach the squadron, do we?"

"No," Angel said unhappily. "This area was considered a safe zone. We have a couple of Irid-ium phones with satellite hookups, but I didn't take one with us. I didn't think we'd need it." Scowling, she muttered, "Dude, that was a stupid decision on my part. I'll never do that again. I'm takin' that phone with me no matter what village I go into from now on. Lesson learned."

"Don't be hard on yourself," Burke said, feeling his adrenaline finally begin to ebb from his blood-stream. "I'm more worried about the Blackhawk coming in at 0800. Will the druggies still be here?"

"I doubt it," Angel said. "Usually, their tactics are to hit and run. They'll land at a village, scare the bejesus outta the inhabitants, and then take off."

Though he could hardly see her in the darkness of the cave, Burke studied her features. "Are you okay?"

"Yeah. Just shook up, is all. How about you?"

"I'd rather be sleeping with you in my arms."

"You're a die-hard romantic, Gifford. We have druggies land on our heads and you're thinking about holding me."

"Do you blame me?"

"No. It's kinda nice."

"Good."

She sat with him, the silence closing around them as the sound from the helicopters faded. Below them, she could hear the burble of the river flowing slowly past. Emotionally, she was in a quandary. Burke's kiss had opened her up like an orchid that bloomed only once every five or seven years. And she'd been the one to initiate it. Rubbing her chest, Angel scowled. "Whatta mess," she muttered.

"What? Us or the druggies landing on our heads?"

"Both."

"We're alive. That's all that counts."

Nodding, Angel peered out the cave entrance. The silvery radiance of the moon made everything look grayish. "I want us to stay that way, too."

"Do you think once the drug soldiers find out there's whooping cough in the village it will scare them off?"

"No. They're probably too stupid to realize the implications of the disease. Most of the soldiers are mercenaries from other countries, not Peruvians. That means they probably have had vaccinations, so they don't have to worry about contracting it."

"You've been dodging and ducking these druggies for the last four years to help villages like this?"

"Yeah. Why?"

Shaking his head, Burke muttered, "I just didn't realize what danger you live in...."

"What?" Angel gave a strangled, soft laugh. "That we're at war 24/7 down here?"

"Yeah..." Burke was unhappy about it, but not for the reasons Angel suspected. Kissing her, holding her in sleep, had made him even more deeply aware of his need for her.

Angel absorbed Burke's bulk and closeness, his quiet strength. He held her hand gently, resting it on top of his long, hard thigh. "We're at war, Burke. Plain and simple. This is a good example of it. You never know when the druggies might strike. They have state-of-the-art helos with highly trained mercs flyin' them. These guys know their business. They'd rather shoot first and ask questions later. They take *no* prisoners."

"When we get out of this mess, can the Peruvian army help Yanatin stay free of druggies?"

"I doubt it," Angel sighed. She closed her eyes and leaned her head on his shoulder. To her delight, Burke released her hand and slid his arm around her, drawing her close. Snuggling her face into the crook of his neck, she said wearily, "Ever since Mike Houston left, the Peruvian army has lost its momentum and focus. When Mike was down here he kept a reign of terror focused on the drug lords. They called him the Jaguar God because he had the nine lives of a cat. He had the druggies on the run, and he freed a lot of villages through his systematic plan of getting the army in there on a regular basis to help them. The drug lords backed away from enslaving a lot of the villages because Mike had helicopter squadrons of soldiers who could drop in and meet them head-on in firefights. Mike rarely lost a battle.''

''But now it's different?'' Burke rested his chin against her soft, silky hair, absorbing the warmth of her body pressed to his. When Angel slid her good arm across his torso, his heart was flooded with such joy that it took him utterly by surprise.

''Very different. Even though the Peruvian army was trained by him and other Special Forces advisors, now that Mike's gone, they haven't got the same focus or desire. He was a helluva charismatic leader and no one has been able to fill his shoes, so its sort of fallen apart.''

''Special Forces men are intense,'' Burke agreed.

''You should know. You're one.'' She muffled her laugh against his shoulder.

Worried, Burke said nothing. Outside, the world seemed peaceful except for the sounds of helicopters far in the distance. He wondered how the villagers were. A part of him wanted to go back there and try to defend them, but he knew a handgun wasn't going to do that. A Kamov could take him out in a second. And he knew druggies were always heavily armed, with the best weapons that could be bought anywhere in the world. No, he'd just be a sitting target to take out. Suddenly, life was valuable as never before to him. With Angel in his arms, her body drawn against his for warmth and protection, he felt a fierce emotion that he knew was love. There was no mistaking it.

Sitting there, his back against the dry wall of the cave, Burke shut his eyes and pondered that miracle. He was falling deeply in love with Angel. And there was nothing he could do about it.

Chapter Nine

Though she was perfectly happy to sleep in Burke's arms, to feel his heart beating against hers, something forced Angel to open her eyes. Lifting her head, she peered intently toward the mouth of the cave. Gasping, she sat up.

"What?" Burke asked, tensing.

"Look!" She jabbed a finger toward the opening.

Eyes widening, Burke saw a golden jaguar with black spots standing at the entrance. The animal was looking at them, its eyes huge and gold, its tail casually flicking from side to side. Without thinking, Burke pulled his pistol from its holster.

"No!" Angel whispered harshly. "Don't shoot him!"

Lowering the weapon, Burke kept his gaze trained on the jaguar. "Why not?"

"Because…" Angel scrambled to her hands and knees "…jaguars don't come out during daylight," she breathed. "They sleep. This is different.…"

Confused and scared, Burke looked at her and then at the huge cat that blocked the cave mouth. Terror ate at him. The animal was only ten feet away! He kept his finger on the trigger of his Beretta even though he wasn't aiming it at the cat. "*How* is this different? That's a wild animal! It could charge us. Kill us."

Holding up her hand, Angel moaned. "Shh! Just be quiet, Burke. Let me think!" Touching her brow, she willed herself to settle down. Her heart was pounding roughly in her chest, the adrenaline making her flighty and nervous.

"What's there to *think* about?" he demanded harshly, getting to his knees.

"This isn't what you think!" Angel hissed in exasperation. "My mother's people all have jaguar spirit guardians. They're our protectors! If something dangerous is comin' down, they show up to warn us.'' She stared out at the jaguar, which stood languidly, the end of its long tail flicking back and forth. Angel felt an unnatural pressure in her head, as if the cat was trying to communicate with her. ''Oh, dammit!'' she whispered, rubbing her brow. Her head felt like it was going to explode. She knew without a doubt the energy of the jaguar was affecting her.

''What can I do?'' Burke asked worriedly when he saw Angel holding her head.

''Let me try and talk to it.''

Stymied by her comment, Burke once again felt like a fish out of water. This place was strange. It was mystical. Mysterious. Unexplainable. He stared disbelievingly at the jaguar—male—which stood there calmly, not threatening them in any way. Burke found that incredible. And impossible.

Angel scrunched up her eyes, her fingers digging into her skull. ''My mother said if a jaguar shows up, there's danger. She said I could talk to it, from my mind to the cat's.''

''Mental telepathy?'' Burke asked, grasping for straws and not really believing such a thing was possible. Yet the cat didn't move. It was now staring intently at Angel.

''Yeah…I think. Hold on…lemme try. I've never done this before. I'm not trained for it. Now I'm

wishing I had let my mother train me. Damn…''
She closed her eyes. Angel didn't know what she
was doing or even how to try. The training would
have given her that knowledge. Right now, she was
scared. Really scared, because a jaguar spirit showing up in physical form meant one thing: death
threats to her and Burke. What did the cat know?
She tried to talk to it, in English and Quechua and
Spanish, but nothing happened. Her head felt full
of energy, like an overfilled balloon that was on the
verge of exploding. There was no pain, thankfully,
just an unmitigating pressure inside her skull.

Finally, she stopped panicking. She stopped trying to communicate. Instead, she grounded herself.
She cleared herself as she would when asking for
healing energy to flow through her to a person in
need. The instant she got out of the way, a scene
flashed behind her closed eyes.

Gasping, Angel's eyes flew open. ''We gotta get
outta here! The druggies! They're huntin' for us!
Someone in the village told them which path we
took.''

Burke's heart contracted. He saw the terror in
Angel's eyes as she drew her pistol. At the same
moment, the jaguar moved away from the entrance,
to let them out.

''How do you know?'' he demanded.

"The cat," Angel whispered fiercely, hurrying toward the mouth of the cave. "It showed me five men comin' our way. They've got assault rifles. We're outgunned, Burke. They know we're here!"

"The cat told you *that*?" he demanded incredulously. Still, he hurried to her side. Once outside the cave, he looked around for the jaguar. There, no more than thirty feet away from them, stood the cat, staring calmly back at them. In front of him footpaths led in six different directions.

"Yes, it *did!* This isn't a time for disbelief, Burke." Angel brushed her hair away from her eyes. Turning, she looked back up the path they'd come on. Her breath halted momentarily. There, at the bend in the trail, she saw the first druggie appear, an assault rifle in hand.

"There they are!"

Burke saw the drug soldiers. They were a quarter of a mile away, up the hill. And it was obvious the men saw them. Instantly, they shouted and raised their weapons.

The air exploded with gunfire. Mounds of dirt shot up around them. Bullets whistled past. Burke cursed, sank down on one knee and returned fire.

Angel saw the jaguar leap ahead and choose one of the paths. Crouching, she turned and grabbed at

Burke's jacket. Giving it a sharp tug, she yelled, "Get up! Follow me!"

Just as Burke leaped up and turned on his heel to follow her, he felt a hot, stinging sensation in his upper arm. Ignoring it, he dug his boots into the soft grass and sprinted after her. Up ahead, to his amazement, he saw the jaguar running ahead of them. This was crazy!

He didn't have time to think about it. Rasping for air, he ran into the darkened jungle, which quickly closed in around them. The bullets stopped. Hearing the shouts of the drug soldiers in hot pursuit, Burke surged ahead. The path led upward, twisting like a writhing snake and wide enough only for one person. The Peruvian jungle was no place for a person to try to hide in. The trees were set too close together and the walls of woody vines were practically impenetrable. All they could do, as far as Burke could see, was follow the footpaths that villagers had carved out by machete a long time ago.

The path they were on forked again, in four different directions. Gasping for air, Burke slowed when Angel did. The jaguar trotted off on another footpath, and she followed it. Where the hell were they going? The cat shouldn't be here! The noise of the rifles should have frightened it off. Something was going on that Burke didn't understand. He saw Angel spin around and look at him, worry etched on her damp, gleaming features.

"Burke!" Her cry startled him. He slowed to a walk as she ran back toward him.

"What?" he gasped, looking back up the trail and seeing the drug soldiers taking the same path. They were still in hot pursuit. The only chance for escape was to take one of these smaller trails and slip down it unseen, so that the druggies would have a harder time figuring out which one they'd taken.

"Oh, no!" Angel whispered. She reached for his left arm. "You're hit!"

"What?" He looked down and felt alarm spread through him. Blood was soaking through the sleeve of his jacket. He'd been wounded in the lower left arm. Blood had trickled down each of his fingers and was dripping into the dirt.

Grabbing his jacket, Angel quickly shoved it upward to expose his dark, hairy forearm. A bullet had pierced it, gone through it. Fear gutted her. It was a clean wound. The only problem was it was spurting blood. That meant an artery had been nicked or severed.

"Put pressure on it, Burke! Hurry! Come on, we gotta get away from the druggies!"

Holstering his pistol, Burke nodded. Pressing his right hand over his left arm, he applied pressure. Because his adrenaline was flowing, he'd felt no pain when the bullet hit. "Let's go," he rasped, turning and looking back. There was no sign of the soldiers. Not yet.

Breathing hard, Angel grabbed him. "You follow the jaguar! I'll stay behind and make sure you're with us." She tried to keep the fear out of her voice. How much blood had Burke lost already? Could they stop the bleeding once they were safe from the soldiers? Her mind spun with questions and with answers she didn't like. Pushing Burke ahead of her on the narrow path, she rasped, "Get going! Follow the cat. He's going to lead us to a safe place...."

Burke didn't argue. The jaguar trotted down a shadowy path that led ever higher on the jungle-clad mountain. Burke saw the cat pick up speed and he followed quickly. Angel was on his heels, her pistol drawn.

Mind spinning, he looked down every once in a while at his wound. The bleeding continued unabated. Scared, because he knew that sooner or later his loss of blood would weaken him and slow them down, he pushed ahead relentlessly. No longer did he doubt the jaguar; the cat seemed to know where it was going. Another half mile up the mountain, the path forked again. Without hesitation, the animal took one branch. Burke followed without argument.

Angel tried to keep her worry at bay. Burke was trotting gamely down a path that seemed to be leading around the top of the mountain, from what she could tell. Every once in a while she'd halt and listen for voices. The jungle was thick and impenetrable, the tree limbs covered with green moss. She heard no voices. Turning, she hurried to catch up with Burke and the jaguar.

Burke began to feel the effects of his loss of blood. He was beginning to stumble over exposed roots that snaked across the dirt path from time to time. They traveled another half hour and he saw the thick walls of jungle beginning to thin out. The jaguar took another path that led down a steep incline. Burke was careful where he placed his feet, feeling dizziness wash over him every few minutes. Compressing his lips, he gathered his eroding strength and pushed on. The path was narrow and rarely used, from what he could tell. It was more like an animal trail than a human one. The trees thinned even more, and up ahead, he saw more light. Knowing that Yanatin stood between the jungle and the grassy lowlands, he wondered if that was where they were going.

Beads of sweat ran down his face. Looking back every once in a while, he saw Angel, pistol in hand, running behind him. Her face was dark with worry.

The jaguar increased its pace. Burke stumbled, caught himself and surged on, suddenly finding himself waist-deep in the lush green grass that grew in the lowlands. The path wound through it, sloping ever downward. After the shadowy jungle, the sunlight was dazzling. The sky was a powdery blue, filled with wispy, low-hanging white clouds.

Feeling his heart pounding in his chest, Burke knew he was weakening. He'd lost too much blood. Knowing he was in trouble, he gritted his teeth and focused on the jaguar as it followed the trail. Up ahead, he saw a huge stand of trees out in the middle of the tall grass, which gently swayed with the inconstant morning breeze. Dewdrops gleamed on every blade. Sunlight would catch them, and Burke would see tiny rainbow hues glint as he ran down the path.

The stand of trees stood like a fortress on the side of a huge hill at least five thousand feet high. Burke stumbled into the grove and stopped. The jaguar stood ten feet in front of him, its mouth open, panting.

Angel jerked to a halt at Burke's side. She looked up at him. His face was ashen. "This is it. This is our hiding place. Come on, you need to sit down so I can look at your wound, Burke." She holstered her pistol and tugged at his right hand, leading him to a huge tree. The roots were like flying buttresses, five to seven feet in height, spread out around the massive truck. Between the roots were dry corners where leaves had collected over the years, forming a soft, spongy seat. Angel led Burke to one of them and helped him to sit down.

Burke didn't fight Angel. He kept his eye on the jaguar, which crouched about twenty feet away from them, near the path they'd just followed. It was as if the cat were guarding them. That's what Burke felt, anyway. Laughing at himself, he decided he was weak from loss of blood and his mind was gyrating crazily with ridiculous thoughts.

"Just relax," Angel rasped, breathing hard, as he helped him lean back against the smooth gray trunk of the towering tree, the green branches of which were splayed out like an umbrella a hundred feet above them. "Get your coat off...." With trembling fingers she helped him unbutton it. Luckily, her left arm was regaining mobility. She still didn't have her usual range of motion, but at least she could help Burke.

Trying to steel herself against what she would find, Angel lay his jacket aside, studying his ashen face, which was covered in sweat. She knew he was in pain, judging by the way his mouth slashed downward. Settling between his opened legs, she took a good look at the bleeding wound on his lower left arm.

"There's an artery cut," he murmured, looking at it with her.

"Yeah...yeah, there is...." She could see the perfect hole where the bullet had plowed through his arm, tearing the tissue. The artery had been torn, and was pumping out blood methodically, with every heartbeat. "And I have nothing with me to stop it."

Hearing the terror in her voice, the frustration, he leaned back. "The only thing we've got right now is direct pressure," he whispered. His world was graying. "Listen, I'm starting to black out," he told her in a low, shaky tone. Burke felt as if he were talking from a tunnel, his voice an echo. He saw Angel's eyes widen and fill with tears. In that moment, he saw so much. He tipped his head back against the trunk of the tree and tried to smile as weakness flowed through him. "I'll be okay, sweetheart." It was a lie. Burke knew that the artery had been clipped in such a fashion that it couldn't automatically close up on its own. The bullet had hit it at such an angle that nothing short of immediate surgery could stop him from bleeding out.

Sobbing, Angel whispered, "Hang on, Burke! Don't you *dare* die on me! You hear me?" She reached forward, examining his wound and her own hands were bloody now as they ran along his hairy flesh. Her tears made his face blurry, but she knew he was on the verge of passing out. Mind spinning, Angel whispered, "I want you to lie down, Burke. *Now!* Do it now! You're going into shock."

It took everything he had to lie down flat on his back. Angel scrambled around and found a small limb. She placed it beneath his feet, to lift them slightly. That was what they did for shock, he realized hazily. When she came back to his side, her face alive with fear and worry, he tried to smile but failed.

"I—I'm sorry, Angel...."

"Shh! There's nothing to be sorry for!" She saw the jaguar sitting on the path, staring at her. What could she do? Oh, how she wished she had the training her mother had! Inca, Maya's sister, was a trained healer of the Jaguar Clan. She could make wounds disappear. Inca knew how to work with her spirit guardian and make it happen. Miracles were a part of Angel's reality, but as she sat at Burke's side, watching his face go gray with loss of blood, her heart burst with such anguish that all she could do was cry.

A movement out of the corner of her eye caught her attention. Lifting her chin, tears trailing down her cheeks, Angel saw the jaguar slowly get up and walk toward her. Gulping, she tensed. Was the cat finally going to attack them? Did he smell the fresh blood and think they were prey? Unsure, she reached for the holster where her pistol was located.

And then something happened. Angel watched the jaguar come within six feet of her and sit down. His gold eyes never left hers. Again she felt pressure building in her head. Gasping for breath, fear streaming through her, she realized he was trying to communicate with her.

It was so hard to quiet her mind right now! Her heart was pounding with anguish. She loved Burke, she realized, even if she'd fought that feeling previously. Angel realized she had been too frightened of the past, of losing a man she loved, to take another chance. Now she knew that had changed. She had changed. Looking down at Burke, whose eyes were barely open, she sniffed. Again the thought that she should clear her mind hit her like a powerful tidal wave.

Closing her eyes, Angel did her best. Her mind

bounced like a yo-yo and the pressure in her head built even more. Trying to steady herself, she visualized tree roots growing from her feet down into the earth, and herself opening up like an empty pipe. The instant she did, she felt her world tip and spin. Placing one hand beneath Burke's wound and her other over top, she took a deep, calming breath.

The jaguar got to its feet, but this time she felt no fear. She had no idea what the cat was going to do, but she had to take a chance.

A feeling of trust washed over her. *Trust.* Her mind spun. Trust what? Burke was bleeding to death. No matter what she did, Angel knew she couldn't save him. She had absolutely no medical tools, no IV to help stabilize him. And then the realization hit her. She had her hands! She had healed before, hadn't she? Well, yes, but nothing like this! And not the man she loved. He was dying right before her eyes. Angel had been so shocked by the unexpected events that she wasn't thinking clearly at all. Under ordinary circumstances, she always remembered to use her hands after she'd done what she could medically for her patient.

Sniffing again, Angel bowed her head and tried to concentrate on staying open. She'd never before experienced the sensations that were now moving through her. She felt as if she were tilting awkwardly, and the urge to open her eyes was very real. But if she did, she knew she'd lose the connection with the jaguar. Intuitively, she understood that the cat was coming closer to help them, not harm them.

And then a powerful warmth began to develop at the top of her head and slowly move downward, enveloping all of her body. It was a steadying sensation. Her fear melted away. Instead, she felt a huge, powerful heart pounding in time with her own. What was happening? She had no idea, but in her desperation, she would try anything, even make herself available to the jaguar, in order to save Burke's life.

Her fingers closed more firmly on his arm. She felt his warm blood leaking between her fingers. More tears flooded her tightly shut eyes as she allowed the powerful energy to pulse through her.

Burke was seeing things, he decided, as he watched the jaguar come within six feet of them. Its huge eyes were trained on Angel. Though Burke knew he should be scared, he wasn't. He knew he was bleeding out. In another minute or two he'd lose consciousness and die. Opening his mouth, he tried to speak, but nothing came out. He was so weak he could no longer make any sound. Desperately, Burke wanted to tell Angel that he loved her. Oh, why had it taken this tragedy to get him to realize it? To accept what he already knew? His heart ached in his chest. Why had he been so stubborn? The moment he'd laid eyes on Angel, he'd known how he felt about her. Damn. It was too late. He was going to die. And he couldn't even muster the words to tell her he loved her.

Just as he closed his eyes, Burke saw that same gray, cottony cloud surround Angel that he'd seen when she'd healed Maria with her hands. Angel knelt at his side, her hands around his wounded arm, her head bowed, eyes tightly shut. Her lips were parted. He saw tears trailing down her glistening cheeks and dripping off her chin, and his heart ached. How much he loved her! And she would never know.

Burke felt tears swimming hotly in his own eyes. For a moment, the world blurred before him. And then he saw something new. The gray, cottony cloud around Angel took form—a familiar shape. He saw the jaguar, fitting around Angel like a glove as she knelt at Burke's side.

That was impossible. He was hallucinating due to blood loss. Yet as he closed his eyes, Burke felt such violent heat come out of Angel's hands and surround the bullet wound in his arm that he gasped. The heat was unlike anything he'd ever experienced. Burke felt as if someone had lit a blowtorch and was holding it to his wound, burning him. It wasn't painful, exactly; just highly uncomfortable. What was going on? Was this what death felt like?

Unable to fight any longer, Burke felt his world slipping away from him. The last thing he heard was Angel softly crying and telling him that she loved him, and that he couldn't die. And then everything went black.

Chapter Ten

Angel lifted her trembling hands from around Burke's bloody arm. She felt the energy shift away from her, and as it left, she began to hear the normal sounds of nature once more. More than anything, she heard the screams of the monkeys, warning her that there were drug soldiers tramping through the jungle, looking for them.

Feeling dizzy, she blinked several times as she looked down at Burke. He'd passed out. Frightened, she stared down at the hole in his arm. No longer was blood pumping out of it. Gasping, Angel bent down and looked at it more closely. How could that be? In disbelief, she examined the wound thoroughly. There was no more bleeding. Taking in a wobbly breath, her heart beating painfully in her chest, she lifted his slack arm and studied the exit wound. No blood. The bleeding had stopped! This was different from her other healing experiences. Before, hemorrhaging or shock would halt. But never had the flesh closed up and healed.

Glancing up, she saw the jaguar sitting five feet away from her, lazily switching its tail as it looked toward the path they had followed earlier. In amazement, Angel gently turned Burke's arm over again and stared at it, then let it rest against his side. Shakily placing two fingers against the carotid artery in his neck, she felt for his pulse. It was weak, but constant. That meant he'd lost a lot of blood, but had stabilized.

"T-thank you," she whispered unsteadily to the jaguar. "Thank you for what you did for him."

The cat swiveled its huge, flat head, studied her for a moment, then turned and watched the trail with new alertness.

Angel felt a sense of danger wash over her. This time, as she ripped a piece of cloth from the bottom of her jacket to make a bandage for Burke's wounded arm, she was certain the jaguar was "talking" to her. Though her fingers shook badly, she managed to place the dressing on Burke's arm and knot it firmly. As she did so, he groaned. Turning, Angel watched as he slowly became conscious. His face was gray, and tense with obvious pain. Wiping her hands on the dew-laden grass, she was able to wash most of his blood from them. After drying them on her thighs, she leaned over and caressed his cheek with her hand.

"Burke? Burke? Wake up. We gotta get outta here. The drug soldiers are coming. Do you hear me? You have to stand. I'll help you...."

Angel's voice sounded faraway, as if she was shouting at him through an echo chamber. Burke was still caught up in what he was seeing behind his closed eyes. As he'd passed out from loss of blood, he'd entered a tunnel of white light. Unsure of where he was, he'd walked toward a figure waiting in the distance for him. As he approached, he saw it was a woman, tall and proud-looking, but very, very old. Her hair was a silvery-gray and bound in two long, thick braids that hung down the front of her light pink gown, over her cream-colored vest. Her watery blue eyes glowed with such love that he felt magnetically drawn to her.

She lifted her hand. "Come no farther, my son."

Burke halted and gazed around, but all he saw

was the tunnel. Turning back, he stared at her. "Who are you?"

"I'm Alaria." She smiled benignly. "One of your guardian angels, Burke." Her lips lifted a little. "I don't have wings, however."

He felt her gentle laughter, rather than heard it. Stymied, he asked, "Where am I?"

"At the threshold, my son. It is a place we all traverse at some point in our lives."

Confused, Burke stared at Alaria. When he did, he saw himself lying sprawled out, unconscious, against the base of a tree. His heart started to pound. He saw Angel leaning over him, holding his bloody arm between her hands and crying. A powerful, jolting feeling moved through him like a tidal wave. He loved her. Unequivocally. But why was she crying? Taking a closer look, he saw the blood on his arm.

"You've been wounded," Alaria told him softly as she moved to his shoulder.

"Yes..."

"That's why you're here, my son. You have a decision to make."

Turning, Burke studied Alaria's serene features. Her face was deeply wrinkled and yet there was such a glowing life emanating from her that she looked much younger than she probably was. "What decision?" he asked.

"To come with me or to go back there," she said, pointing toward where he lay, with Angel at his side.

The pull to go with Alaria was strong, there was no doubt. Burke absorbed the love that came from her and surrounded him. Yet, as he turned on his heel and looked at Angel, whose face was glistening with tears over him, his heart lurched with such a fierce love for her that he said, "I want to go back, Alaria. I love her. I want time with her. Is that all right?"

Alaria smiled gently. "Of course it is, my son. Our life consists of many windows of opportunity. Coming across the threshold is up to you. Your chosen path on earth is not yet completed, and it's a wise choice you've made." She lifted her hand toward him, palm outward. "Turn around and I'll send you back."

He hesitated. "You're an angel?"

She smiled fully. "You may call me that if you want. I am one of your guardians. You have many. I wanted to meet you here today to let you know that you are greatly loved on this side and that someday, we will welcome you across. Go back now, my son. Fulfill your destiny."

Then it was as if everything suddenly speeded up around him. Burke felt himself spiraling down the tunnel. He lost sight of his guardian angel and closed his eyes. As he spun downward, he felt heavier and heavier, until he felt almost as if he were in encased in concrete.

Forcing his eyes open, he found that everything was blurred. He heard Angel's voice, low and tense, speaking to him. "Burke? Burke! Wake up! We gotta go! The drug soldiers are near!"

The urgency in her voice spurred him to action. Though he was terribly weak, he forced himself to sit. Blinking, he tried to reorient himself. Angel was on her feet, tugging hard on his arm trying to get him to move. Sounds of the jungle began to register on his senses, as did the fragrance of grass and other vegetation. Struggling, Burke lurched unsteadily to his feet. The moment he did, he felt light-headed. If Angel hadn't quickly stepped close, pulling his arm around her small shoulders, he would have fallen on his nose. Leaning heavily against her, Burke shook his head to clear it. His vision improved by the minute. As she led him, stumbling, out of the grove, he saw the jaguar ahead of them.

"This is crazy," he muttered, his words slurring.

"Shh!" Angel hissed, absorbing his weight and

guiding him through the thick, wet grass. "Don't talk. Just concentrate on putting one foot in front of another!"

Burke had no idea how long they walked. It seemed like forever. And with every step, he felt a little weaker. The memory of his vision of Alaria warred with the reality of where he was now. He felt as if he was in two places at once, and not fully in either.

The jungle canopy closed in over them as they left the grassy lowlands behind. The path was full of exposed roots, and Burke concentrated hard on stepping over them, to keep from falling. Sweat popped out on his face and ran down it. His breathing was labored. The pain in his arm was red-hot and throbbing. But it cleared his mind, brought him fully back into his body.

Huffing, Angel gripped Burke, her arm tightly wrapped around his waist. He clung to her shoulders as she guided him deeper and deeper into the forest. Her mind spun with possibilities. She knew that at 0800 today, the Blackhawk was to come back with more medical supplies. It was 0600 now. What if the druggies were still there when the Blackhawk arrived? She worried that the Kamov Black Shark helicopter would shoot the Blackhawk down. Yet there was no way to warn the BJS base. She hadn't brought a satellite phone.

The jaguar led them to a small, shallow stream. The trail continued on up the opposite bank. Angel hesitated at the shore. The jaguar looked at her, obviously encouraging her to follow as it stepped into the water and moved downstream. It was a good idea. The drug soldiers were first-rate trackers, judging by the way they'd managed to trail their prey into the lowlands. But the soldiers wouldn't be able to track them through the water. Moving into the ankle-deep stream, which was clear and placid, Angel and Burke splashed along unsteadily.

Burke felt weaker and weaker as they made their way downstream. He had no idea how long they staggered through the water, dodging thick foliage that grew on the banks. More and more, he leaned on Angel. She was small but strong, he discovered. He could see her profile and the stubborn look on her face.

They continued for more than thirty minutes down the winding stream until it led to the edge of the jungle once more. In this part of the forest a lot of jagged black rocks stood up like fortresses here and there, and long grasses lined the stream. The screaming warning of the monkeys faded behind them. Studying the grass, Angel realized the soldiers would easily find their trail here; it would be impossible not to see it, once the stems were trampled by their footsteps. As they rounded a curve in the stream, she saw a huge fortress of black lava on their right. To her delight, she spotted a cave within it. Ahead, the jaguar stepped out of the water onto the rocky bank and trotted up to the mouth of the cave.

Receiving a strong impression from the jaguar that this was the end of their journey, Angel helped Burke as he floundered out of the creek. Though their boots were waterproof, creek water had sloshed over the tops, and their feet were soaked. The temperature hovered around sixty-five degrees, with wispy fog hanging at the top of the canopy as usual.

"This is our new home," Angel whispered, out of breath as she helped Burke climb the stony slope toward the cave.

"Good," he muttered. "I don't think I can take another step...."

"Me neither," she gasped. She led him to the cave mouth, where he sank to his knees. "Crawl in there, Burke. Get to the back where no one can see you. I'm going to go back to the stream and try to cover our tracks. Just in case."

Once inside, Burke collapsed at the back on his

belly, his good arm beneath his cheek. The last of his strength ebbed away, and he couldn't move another inch. His arm was throbbing with pain, but he no longer cared. Closing his eyes, he rested.

Angel quickly broke a branch from a nearby palm and used it to sweep the stream bank, erasing their bootprints. Feeling shaky from the long trek, she turned and climbed toward the cave. The jaguar was lying just outside of it, licking his paw. Crouching down, she saw Burke lying on his stomach, unmoving. Alarmed, Angel scrambled toward him. By now she'd lost her fear of the jaguar. The cat didn't even look up as she crawled past. The cave would hide them well from prying eyes.

Burke's face was ashen. She placed two fingers on the inside of his wrist. There! His pulse was strong and constant. Angel brushed his dark hair off his brow, which was plastered with sweat. He had either passed out or was sleeping; she wasn't sure which. As Angel knelt there, chewing on her lower lip, she once again felt the presence of the jaguar, like a powerful sensation moving through her. She was beginning to get used to it. There was a feeling of reassurance from the cat about Burke's condition. He was resting; that was all.

Angel wished mightily for her medical bag. She needed a blood pressure cuff so she could see how bad off he really was. Looking around, Angel felt safe in the small, narrow cave, which was roughly five feet high and ten feet deep. It was dry, and that was good.

She had to get help. But how? Kneeling there in the cave, her hands on her thighs, she considered their dilemma. Right now, the druggies were still out there, hunting for them. They'd landed at Yanatin in the middle of the night, and she hadn't heard them take off yet. Looking at her watch, she noted it was 0630. In less than two hours, the BJS Blackhawk would fly in, its pilots unaware of the danger that awaited.

Worry eating at her, Angel stared down at Burke. He was sleeping soundly, his breathing shallow and slow. What was she going to do? The lives of two BJS pilots were on the line. And she needed immediate help for Burke.

Angel was torn. As she looked up, she saw the jaguar come and lie directly in front of the cave entrance. His massive head lifted, and she saw his gold eyes settle on her. She received a distinct impression that the drug soldiers would leave before the Blackhawk helicopter arrived at the village.

Relief surged through her, followed by exhaustion. Her muscles aching from holding Burke up for so long as they crossed the rugged terrain, then splashed down the stream, Angel stretched out behind him. Lying against his back, she closed her eyes. She desperately needed to sleep, too.

She felt the jaguar touch her mind. It was a warm and loving feeling. Face pressed against Burke's back, Angel slid her hand across his waist and closed her eyes. *Safe*. They were finally safe.

As weariness claimed her, Angel fell into a vivid, colorful dream. She saw the jaguar get up and approach her. He wanted to take her somewhere. Without speaking, he told her to get on his back, as if she could ride the cat like a horse! Angel's mind warred with that possibility. In the next instant, she saw the jaguar grow three times his normal size, and she found herself sitting astride him. He sprang into the air, and she was flying through the sky as they raced at top speed to an unknown destination. Angel clung to his neck and hung on. She could feel the warm fur bunched between her hands, the graceful, sinuous movements of the cat between her legs. It was a wild, free feeling, and laughter bubbled up in Angel's throat. Below her, she saw the jungle racing by in a blur of green. Above her, the sky was a light blue, with puffs of white, cottony clouds here and there. The warmth of the sun felt good to her, because she had been so chilled before.

The ride on the jaguar was thrilling. Scary. Euphoric. Ahead, Angel recognized a familiar black, loaf-shaped mountain—where the BJS base was located! The moment she realized that, she found herself standing in Maya Stevenson's office. The cat had disappeared.

Maya looked up, frowning. Stunned, Angel gazed around and then back at her C.O. How had this happened?

"What's wrong, Angel? Why are you here?"

Maya could see her! Angel tried to find her voice. Opening her hands, she haltingly explained the situation. She left nothing out regarding the drug soldiers, the helicopters and the danger awaiting the Blackhawk at Yanatin. When she was done, she felt something large and warm brush against her left leg. Looking down, Angel saw the jaguar. He telepathically told her to get on him once again; it was time to go back.

Angel had only to think it and it occurred. Maya's office dissolved into nothingness in her dream. Within seconds, they were in the sky again, racing along, the wind in her face, the warmth of the sun soaking into her. Within seconds, Angel saw herself sleeping at Burke's side once more. And then darkness claimed her.

* * *

Burke groaned and lifted his weighted lids. His senses sluggish, he lay on his belly, his arm beneath his cheek. Where was he? Feeling slightly better, he slowly rolled onto his good side. There was a small fire at the front of the cave. Rubbing his eyes as he sat up, cross-legged, he realized that Angel was leaning over the fire and holding something on a skewer over the flames.

''Angel?'' His voice was rusty and thick with disuse.

Angel heard Burke croak out her name. She turned and looked toward the back of the cave. He was sitting up, his wounded arm resting on his thigh.

''How are you feeling?''

''Like hell... Where are we, Angel?''

She laughed a little and pulled the fish that she'd been cooking off the flames. ''I don't know. A safe place, that's for sure.''

''What time is it?'' he muttered, lifting his wrist and looking closely at the dials of his watch. A little past 1500, or 3:00 p.m. He watched as Angel crawled back toward him, holding the roasted fish on its skewer.

''Time to eat,'' she said breathlessly. She sat facing him, so that their knees almost touched. Holding up the fish, she said, ''This is dinner. That little stream has a pool about a hundred feet from here, and I was able to catch two big fish, scooping them out onto the bank with my hands.'' She studied Burke's grizzled face. His flesh was pasty-looking, and his eyes were dark. ''How are you feeling?''

''Like hell.'' One corner of his mouth lifted. ''But I'm alive.'' He reached out and touched her cheek. ''And so are you. That's what counts.''

Shaken by his touch, Angel said, ''You need to eat, Burke. You've got to get some of your strength back. You lost a lot of blood.''

Looking at his wrapped arm, he muttered, ''Did it stop bleeding finally?''

''Yeah…it did.'' Angel broke off some of the flaky fish with her fingers. ''Here, eat this. We'll talk later, okay?''

Not having the strength to argue, Burke took the tender white meat and chewed hungrily. With every bite, he felt his stomach purr with gratitude. Slowly, he felt some of his old strength beginning to return. Outside the cave, he heard monkeys calling to one another. Frogs and crickets sounded nearby. He felt safe. After he'd finished the fish, he sat with his back against the wall. Holding his wounded arm against him, he watched as Angel crawled back to the fire. The smoke was rising outside of the cave, but the heat radiated inward and he felt warmed by the flames.

"Won't that smoke draw the drug soldiers?" he asked her. Angel was putting another fish on the skewer. She placed it so that the fish hung over the flames, with rocks to keep it in place.

"They're gone," she said as she crawled back into the cave. Kneeling in front of him, she gently eased his arm away from his body. "They left this morning, around 0700. I saw them when they topped the jungle cover. It was a transport helo and a Kamov Black Shark."

"That's good," Burke murmured, relieved. He watched as Angel gently unwrapped the bloody dressing from around his arm. "How's it look?"

She peered at the wound in the inconstant light from the fire. "Not a pretty sight, but you're not bleeding. That's what's important right now."

"Good," he whispered.

"Just hold it against you, Burke. I'm going to wash this cloth in the stream and get rid of the blood. Hang on...." Angel quickly crawled out of the cave and walked down the slope toward the stream.

Burke sighed, tipped his head back against the wall and closed his eyes. The roasted fish had tasted delicious. He could feel the food being turned into energy in his body. The weakness he'd felt before was receding by degrees. Mind spinning, he heard Angel splashing about, and washing the cloth in the stream. Opening his eyes, Burke peered out the cave. Where was the jaguar? Or had he imagined the whole thing? Unsure, he waited until Angel returned to his side.

"At least this is clean," she murmured, expertly rewrapping his wound, knotting the cloth so that it would stay in place. "Are you thirsty?"

"Yeah, I am. Is the water in the stream any good?"

She smiled a little. "No, you can't trust it. But there're some vines nearby that contain good water. I can break a couple of them off. Hold on and I'll bring you some."

Touching her hand, Burke whispered, "You saved my life, Angel...."

Gripping his fingers, she said, "No, I didn't. The jaguar did...but we'll talk about that after I get you water. Okay?"

So it wasn't a dream, Burke thought, rummaging through his spongy mind and trying to make sense of all he'd seen and heard earlier. When Angel returned ten minutes later, she had several woody vines with her. He tipped the end of the first one up to his mouth and found the water that ran out to be pleasant tasting—slightly acrid, but good.

"More?" Angel asked, kneeling at his side.

"No...I'm fine."

"Really?" She managed a slight smile. Now that Burke had food and water in him, he looked much better. His beard darkened his features and accentuated his cheekbones and large, gray eyes. How she loved him! Angel tried to keep her emotions at bay, but it was almost impossible. Picking up the other vines, she crawled over and placed them outside the cave, because they could tip over and spill out into the narrow confines of the cave. Then she threw more wood on the fire. The warmth made the cave drier and it was more than welcome compared to the humid air outside.

"Come here," Burke whispered, holding out his good hand to her. "Come and let me hold you?"

Tears flooded Angel's eyes. Startled by her reaction, she quickly moved to Burke's side and settled beneath his proffered arm. Being careful not to jostle him or his wounded forearm, Angel slid her hand across his torso.

"I really needed this," she confided, her voice trembling. "I need you, Burke...."

Kissing her mussed hair, he whispered, "Angel,

I love you. I never got a chance to say it before, but I will now.''

His words moved her as nothing else had in her life. Giving him a gentle squeeze, Angel nuzzled against his rock-hard jaw. ''I love you, too, Burke. I was so afraid to admit it. These last twenty-four hours have ripped away all the BS I was fooling myself with. I've been attracted to you since the day you came to the base. I just didn't want to admit it.''

Pressing another kiss to her hair, Burke closed his eyes and held her gently against him. ''Sweetheart, you hit me over the head the moment I laid eyes on you.'' He gave a husky laugh. ''It was mutual I guess.''

''You, too?'' Angel looked up into his shadowed face. His gray eyes were alive with humor and love—for her.

''Yeah, me, too. This attack made me realize I was pretty stupid for not owning up to how I felt.''

Caressing his sandpapery jaw with her fingertips, Angel whispered, ''You probably worried I'd be another Mary Jo.''

''No,'' he countered quietly, ''you were never anything like her, Angel. The complete opposite. I was scared. I'd worked hard over the years not to feel for any woman beyond a certain point, but you melted all my barriers like they weren't there. It left me feeling vulnerable. I didn't know what to do.''

Nodding, Angel rested her head against his shoulder and wrapped her arm around his torso once more. The flames flickered red and yellow light around the dark cave. ''I was scared for different reasons, Burke. I knew you'd leave me. I didn't want to give you my heart and have you walk out a month later.''

''I understand,'' he murmured. How he ached to love Angel, to make her his in every way. There was no way right now, and Burke understood that. ''I don't have any answers for that, either.''

Sadness blanketed Angel. ''Maybe I need to learn to love people while they're with me, and then let them go when it's time. I dunno....''

Hearing the confusion and hurt in her voice, he whispered, ''Listen to me, will you? Let's just get out of this jam first, okay? If this has taught me nothing else, it's shown me that life is full of mystery, full of surprises.'' His mouth quirked. ''First things first. I've got to get help for this wound. If infection sets in, I could die.''

''I know that,'' Angel murmured worriedly. ''Tomorrow morning I'm going to find my way back to the village. You'll stay here, because you're too weak to walk. I've got enough fish for you, and enough firewood stacked outside the cave so that you can eat and stay warm. I'll collect more of the vines so you'll have a water source.'' Angel belatedly realized that she hadn't told Maya where they were located. New at this turn in her paranormal abilities, she was glad she at least warned off the Blackhawk.

Nodding, Burke whispered, ''Sounds like a good plan, sweetheart. For now, though, let's just hold one another? That's what I need—you. We almost died out there. I feel like I got a second chance and I'm taking it—with you.''

Chapter Eleven

Angel didn't want to wake up. She felt Burke's arm around her, and it was a wonderful, comforting feeling—one she realized she had missed terribly during the past five years of her life. Rousing herself, she lifted her head from where it rested on Burke's shoulder, and saw him studying her through half-closed eyes. It was morning; the dull light of dawn was filtering into the cave, where they lay near the rear wall. Hearing the chatter of monkeys and birds, she raised her hand and drowsily scrubbed her eyes.

"How are you?" she asked, quickly easing out

of his embrace and sitting up. Searching Burke's
bearded face, Angel could see that he was still
weak. The red rims of his eyes told her he hadn't
slept much last night, even though she had.

Giving her a slight, crooked smile, Burke rasped,
"I've been better."

Alarmed, Angel reached out, pressing her hand
to his brow. "Fever?" That was the one thing she
was afraid of. If Burke was getting feverish, that
meant his wound had become infected, which could
spell worse trouble for him. They were out in the
middle of the jungle without any antibiotics. Angel
knew that this morning she'd have to find her way
back to the village. There were no phones there, but
perhaps she could meet the Blackhawk helicopter
that would surely return again, looking for them.

"No, no fever. Not yet, at least," Burke whispered. Gazing into her worried brown eyes, he lifted
his hand and threaded his fingers through her
mussed hair, gently taming it back into place. "I've
wanted to touch your hair ever since I met you. Do
you realize that?" Seeing Angel's eyes turn soft
and warm, Burke caressed her cheek. "I like touching you, sweetheart."

Pressing her hand against his, Angel closed her
eyes and whispered, "I like the way you touch me,
Burke."

"Still scared?"

"Yeah. You?"

"Yeah, but since getting shot and having all these crazy, unexplained things going on, I don't care so much anymore." Burke tried to smile, but his weak state made it impossible. Allowing his hand to drop back into his lap, he looked past Angel. "Where's our guard cat? Do you see him around?"

Angel turned on her knees and peered out of the cave. "I don't know. Hold on, I'll go look...." And she crawled out on her hands and knees.

Getting up, she dusted off her knees and the back of her pants. The glade was beautiful this morning, filled with the melodic sounds of the stream trickling past and birds singing. Looking around, Angel didn't see the jaguar. Inhaling deeply, she could smell the faint, spicy fragrance of orchids that grew among the trees nearby.

"Get a move on, Paredes," she muttered to herself. First things first. The fire was almost out. Quickly gathering small twigs and branches, she placed them strategically over the glowing coals. Almost immediately, they caught and flared to life. Adding a few heavier limbs, Angel then went about retrieving more vines that contained water. It was important that Burke not get dehydrated. He'd lost a terrible amount of blood, and since they had no IV to replace the lost fluids, drinking a lot of water was the next best thing. Bundling the vines in her arms, Angel crawled back into the cave. Burke was lying on his back, his eyes closed. Concerned, she scooted over to him, placing the vines within his reach.

"Burke? You okay?" She put her fingers on his pulse, finding it weak but constant. His flesh was pasty-looking. When he opened his eyes and stared up at her, she smiled and brushed several strands of dark brown hair off his brow.

"Yeah...just tired, sweetheart. Bone tired."

"I don't wonder why. You've probably lost close to two pints of blood. Listen, I've got you plenty of water to drink, with these vines." She pointed to them. "I'm going to go down to the pool, try and scoop up more fish, then roast them over the fire. After that, I need to find my way back to the village. I've got to get you help."

Nodding, Burke closed his eyes. "Sounds like a plan. Sorry I'm not much help right now. I don't like feeling useless."

Leaning over, Angel pressed a chaste kiss to his wrinkled brow. "Oh, you men are all alike, loving the lap of luxury we women create for you." She chuckled. When she saw the corners of his mouth move upward slightly, hope flared within her. How much she loved Burke! The feeling was strong and clear, clean through her heart. This incident had ripped away any pretensions she'd had, any games she might consider playing. He'd almost died. If it weren't for the magic of the jaguar, and all the other things that had happened that Angel didn't pretend to understand, she knew she wouldn't be kneeling beside him and talking with him now. He'd be dead.

That sobering thought spurred her to action. "Stay put, Burke. I'm on a roll. Fish first, and then going for help. Just rest." She squeezed his shoulder gently.

The sun had risen higher, sending shafts of light through the triple canopy. Two large, five-pound fish were cooking over the flames of the campfire. Angel had cut off some palm fronds for plates while the fish roasted. With a stick, she flaked off the well-done pieces of fish onto a frond, the white flesh steaming in the coolness of the morning. Above her the thick white clouds were beginning to burn off, leaving patches of blue sky. The blanket of fog formed every night and midmorning would begin to burn off in the strong equatorial sunlight. Quickly flaking the flesh of the second fish onto a palm leaf, she scooped it up and took it to Burke, who had just awakened and was now sitting against the cave wall.

"Breakfast," she murmured with a grin, placing the large frond on his lap. "Not exactly eggs, bacon and coffee. But eat up!"

"Thanks," he murmured, grateful for her care.

Hurrying out, Angel brought back the second palm frond. She sat next to Burke, quickly eating the steaming, flaky fish. She was starved and would need the energy for the trip back to the village. Noticing that Burke was picking disinterestedly at his share, she murmured, "I know you probably don't feel like eating, but you have to, Burke."

"I know…. But all I feel like doing is sleeping."

"Loss of blood makes you that way. Eat," Angel ordered sternly, "and then you can sleep."

"Such a mother hen," he teased, and held her worried gaze. As exhausted as he was, Burke felt a fierce love for Angel welling up in his chest.

Feeling heat steal into her face, Angel smiled at him. "I guess I am. Elizabeth says that, too. I like helping people. It makes me feel good."

"Yeah," Burke said, forcing himself to eat. "Being a paramedic makes my day, too."

Sunlight splashed across the breadth of the stream outside the cave. Angel watched as sunbeams danced like glittering jewels across the gently flowing water. "Speaking of that," she murmured, finishing her fish and then wiping her fingers on the thighs of her jeans, "once we get home, back to BJS, you're going to have an awfully interesting report to write up for the U.S. Army, aren't you?"

Mouth quirking, Burke said, "Yeah, I've been thinking about that." Lifting his bandaged arm, he said, "How the hell do I tell them what you did? That a cut artery healed itself? That I stopped bleeding out?"

Shrugging, Angel said, "That's your problem, Gifford." She grinned widely. Lifting her hand, she gestured toward the mouth of the cave. "One thing you find out about South America real fast is that it's a magical place compared to North America. Maya once said something that made a lot of sense to me."

"What was that?" Burke downed the last of his fish and handed the palm leaf to Angel.

Getting to her knees, she said, "Medically speaking, the human brain is comprised of two hemispheres—right and left. Maya said she was taught that the right brain is our creative, mystical and magical portion. Our left side is our third-dimensional, reality part, the hemisphere we use every day to survive in this world."

"Okay, I can buy that. But where are you going with this?"

"She said if you were standing like a giant in the Pacific Ocean, looking at the two continents, that South America symbolically represented our right brain, the mystical connections to something greater than ourselves and our everyday reality. And North America represents our left brain, concerned with surviving, making money, putting food on the table and having security."

Thinking about it, Burke nodded. "Okay, I can sort of see the comparison. North America is the richest industrial nation on earth. The U.S.A. is concerned with making money, having security and so on."

"Here in South America," Angel told him, "we have history that is thousands of years old and that is tied to Mother Earth. We are raised to believe that the mystical part of our life is as real and essential as is having a job and making money." Gesturing toward the entrance, where the sunlight was growing stronger by the moment, she added, "Down here, Burke, we accept that miracles can happen around us every day." She looked down at his bound arm. "I've laid hands on people before, but I never witnessed anything like what happened to you. I'm grateful it occurred. I can't explain how it happened. I only know it did.''

Angel gave him a slight smile. ''That's what I love about South America—we don't disbelieve things we can't explain, as North Americans do. I see the questions in your eyes and I see you trying to figure it all out.'' Shrugging, she made her way to the entrance. ''Down here, we don't ask 'why.' We simply accept that magic is a part of our every-day reality.''

''And North Americans don't?'' Burke watched as she tossed the palm fronds into the crackling fire.

Turning, Angel nodded. ''Yeah, that about sums it up.'' She held up her hands. ''No one told me I couldn't heal with my hands. In your culture, you were never taught to think that you could. And yet you did. Look at that little girl you held. You *felt* the energy in your hands, Burke. And you listened to her lungs before and afterward. You can't say it didn't happen, and that she wasn't better because of it.''

Nodding, he muttered, ''I know that. I just never expected all this…mystery.'' Managing a twisted smile, he added, ''Does everyone at BJS do what you do?''

Shaking her head, Angel said, "No. Most of the pilots are *norteamericanos* or Europeans."

"Left-brained? Therefore, not believing in magic and mystery?"

"Exactly. Although—" Angel grinned mischievously "—they all know that Maya is *different*. They've flown with her, seen her use her intuition, witnessed how she knows something that's impossible to know. So they've gotten used to her abilities."

"So what would you call her?"

"Looking for the right words to put in your report?" Angel laughed.

"Yeah, I guess I am."

"Paranormal. Your own government employs remote viewers, which is a paranormal skill. So while the official policy might be we don't believe in this, they *are* using it in secret. Are you worried that if you write the truth in your report, they'll laugh you out of the army?"

"Sort of," Burke murmured. "I'd just like to understand it better than I do. So I can defend it with my superiors when I go home."

Rubbing her hands together, Angel said, "Well, first things first. I'm going to the village. We need to get you help today."

"A practical consideration, not a magical one,"

Burke teased gently. Seeing her eyes fill with laughter, he found himself wanting to kiss her again. And again.

''Yeah, well, real life intrudes rather nastily into our magical reality from time to time,'' she noted wryly, and crawled outside the cave and got to her feet.

Burke was just going to lie down again when he heard the familiar whapping of helicopter blades. At first the sound was muted and faraway. He saw Angel halt halfway down the rocky slope to the stream and look upward, searching the sky.

''Angel?'' His voice was weak, but fear made him call out to her. What if it was the druggies again? Were they returning?

''I hear 'em,'' she called. Looking up, she saw that the clouds were thinning rapidly, leaving gaping holes of pale blue sky. There were two helicopters, both coming their way. Gulping, Angel hurried back up the slope and slid far enough into the cave mouth so that her body warmth would not be picked up on infrared. Immediately, she began throwing dirt on the fire to put it out. If it was a Kamov Black Shark, it would locate the flames in seconds. Heart pounding hard, she scooped up huge handfuls of the moist earth to pile on the fire.

Within minutes the blaze was out, though thin white tendrils of smoke still funneled upward.

The choppers were drawing very near. Mouth dry, Angel felt fear snake through her. The helos seemed to be zeroing in on them. About two hundred feet from the cave was a small meadow, large enough to allow a helicopter to land. That didn't make Angel feel any better about things. Drawing her pistol, she made sure the safety was flipped off. Turning, she saw Burke's darkening features. He'd already drawn his pistol and sat waiting.

Burke caught the first glimpse of a helicopter moving slowly toward them at treetop level. He gasped. "It's a Blackhawk!"

In disbelief, Angel leaped out of the cave and holstered her pistol. The helicopter was going to land in the grassy meadow, and as she watched it, joy swept through her. Turning, she grinned at Burke. "Stay here! They're from the Black Jaguar Base! I'll be right back!" and she took off at a dead run toward the meadow. Somehow Angel knew as she ran toward the meadow that Maya had located them with her well-known paranormal abilities. She had sent the helos in to rescue them. How Maya had accomplished this, Angel didn't know. It was a gut feeling she had as she raced through the jungle toward the opening in the jungle.

Shaking his head, Burke wondered how the hell the BJS had known where they were. It was impossible. As he felt the vibrations of the helicopter as it hovered overhead, relief flowed through him. Right now, he didn't care. They were saved! He'd get the medical help he needed.

Closing his eyes, he took in a ragged breath. This was a helluva situation. His mind spun with many questions and no easy answers. But he and Angel would be safe. Safe and alive. Life had never looked so good as it did right now.

"Sergeant Gifford," Elizabeth Cornell said, standing at his bedside in the hospital portion of the medical Quonset hut, "I think you're going to live." She smiled.

Angel stood on the other side of the bed, still in her dirty clothes.

"That's good news, Doctor." Burke looked at the new, clean bandage over his forearm. In his other arm was an IV line giving him the antibodies and fluids he so desperately needed. After their rescue, he'd been brought in by stretcher to the dispensary. Elizabeth had checked his arm, given him a tetanus shot and asked if he'd like to take a hot shower first before she cleaned up his wound. Nothing had sounded better to him. He was also given a pint and a half of whole blood. Now dressed in a blue hospital gown and lying in bed with several pillows propping him up, Burke felt like he'd gone to heaven.

"I thought you'd like to know that the bullet wound is halfway healed," Elizabeth noted, one eyebrow raised. She sat down on a stool next to the bed, clipboard in hand as she wrote her notes. "You have full use of all your fingers, so the bullet didn't destroy any nerves. You're very lucky."

Nodding, Burke said, "Yes, ma'am, I am. What else did you see?" His curiosity was eating him up. He saw her brush tendrils of red hair away from her brow.

Elizabeth looked up and smiled at him. "Magic."

Angel chuckled. Even unshaven, Burke looked much better now. Touching his damp hair, she smoothed it into place across his skull. "There's that operative word—again...."

Giving her a warm look, Burke murmured, "I guess I'd better start getting used to it."

"Around here," Elizabeth said primly, getting up and closing the clipboard, "it's a daily part of our existence."

"So I've been informed," he said, sharing a warm look with Angel. Then he turned and searched the doctor's green eyes, which danced with deviltry and humor. "Did you have trouble reconciling traditional medicine with…well, this other type of medicine, Doctor?"

Elizabeth smiled benignly. "Sergeant, let's save this conversation for another time, shall we? You just got back to BJS an hour ago. You need your sleep." Looking over at Angel, she said, "And you need to get cleaned up and into a fresh set of clothes. Major Stevenson asked you to drop by when you could, as soon as things settled down around here."

"Yes, ma'am, I'll do that." Angel reached out and touched Burke's shoulder. His eyes were already half-closed. "I'll check in on you later, Burke."

Giving her a slight smile, he murmured, "I'd like that…." He wasn't sure how much he could say around the medical officer. Normally, no one in the military was allowed to show warm feelings or affection toward another. Not wanting to put Angel in jeopardy, Burke said nothing more. The look in her dark eyes, however, told him she loved him. It gave him a helluva good feeling as he watched her walk toward the door.

"She'll be back sooner rather than later, I think," Elizabeth told him in a confidential tone as she moved the stool back against the wall. "Just sleep, Sergeant. Sleep is the great healer. I'm not going to send you to the hospital in Cuzco. Your arm is well on its way to mending, and no surgery, as far as I can see, needs to be performed. Later maybe, but not now."

"Yes, ma'am. Thanks for your help. I was glad to get back here."

"We were all worried about you." She leaned down and touched his shoulder. "Get some rest."

"Doctor?" he called.

Elizabeth hesitated. "Yes?"

"My arm…do you know how it happened? I had a torn artery that was shooting blood with every pump of my heart. I should have bled out. Did Angel tell you that she put her hands over it?"

Shaking her head, Elizabeth said primly, "Sergeant, let it go. Don't try and figure out the how and why of it. This isn't the first time Angel has saved a life that shouldn't have been saved. Over the years, I've come to accept that there are miracles out there—miracles I don't even begin to understand. I don't even try to figure it out anymore. If it's our time to go, we're going to go. But sometimes it isn't, and that's when, from time to time, I see intervention—on the part of someone and some *thing*—work around here." She shook her head.

"Life, I've discovered, is truly mysterious and mystical. Angel made me a believer in the use of hands-on healing a long time ago." She pointed to his swathed arm. "This is the first time I've seen this, however."

"What?" he demanded.

Putting the clipboard on the end of the bed and placing her hands in the pockets of her lab coat, Elizabeth said, "Actual healing of the tissue. Your wound is fifty percent healed, Sergeant. There's no way that could or should have happened in less than forty-eight hours. You just had a bullet rip through your arm. It shouldn't have healed this quickly. It's a medical impossibility."

"No," Burke murmured. "You're right."

She smiled slightly. "Puts you between a rock and a hard place, doesn't it? Aren't you down here on a fact-finding mission to discover just how we deal with deep-tissue trauma out in the middle of a jungle, with no hospital nearby?"

"Yes, ma'am, I am."

"I'd say you have your work cut out for you." Elizabeth moved to the door and opened it. "And I'm glad I don't have to be the one to write your report."

Frowning, Burke said, "How would you write it?"

"Tell the truth, Sergeant. That's what you're charged with doing. That's why you came down here. You serve no one and nothing by not reporting what actually happened."

He nodded, agreeing with her. "I'll tell the truth, Doctor."

"Good. The problem, as I see it, is in how your superiors are going to react to it."

Once the door shut behind the doctor, tiredness swept over Burke. He closed his eyes. Elizabeth's worrisome words were the last he heard as he spiraled into a very deep, healing sleep. But the last face he saw in his mind's eye was Angel's. He drowned in the warmth of her eyes, which smiled back at him.

An incredible sense of peace blanketed Burke. Loving Angel was like breathing. She had become an integral part of his life. How was he going to reconcile that with his duties to the army? In less than four weeks, he was due to rotate back to the U.S.A.—without her.

Chapter Twelve

"Sergeant Gifford," Major Stevenson said as she leaned back in her chair, her fingers propped together in a steeple, "you have a choice."

Burke stood at parade rest in front of her office desk. "Ma'am?" He searched her calm face, mesmerized as always by her large emerald eyes, which seemed alive with mystery. In the last month, since he'd come back from his brush with death, he'd heard more and more tidbits about this woman who ran BJS. And this was the second time he'd had quality time with her. The last time was the day he'd been brought in from the jungle, wounded.

Maya had visited for a few minutes to check up on him, to see how he was getting along and if he needed anything. Yes, she was a good leader, no doubt. Now, as he stood before her, his hands behind his back, he wondered what this was all about.

Opening her hands, Maya said, "You have a choice, Sergeant. I understand from Angel that you've been working long, laborious hours on your report for the higher-ups in the medical corps of the U.S. Army on what you've seen and experienced down here."

"Yes, ma'am, I have." He saw her mouth twitch, a sparkle come to her eyes. Maya's black hair was thick and framed her face, falling across the shoulders of her black flight uniform.

"Did you tell the truth?"

Burke blinked. "The truth?"

"Yes."

"I did, ma'am. *All* of it. Even the parts I don't pretend to understand, figure out or explain."

"Good," she murmured, pleased. "My money was on you to call the shots on this, Gifford."

"I don't dodge bullets, ma'am. This was a factfinding mission. I'd like to think I have an open mind, and that I'm nonjudgmental about what I observe or experience."

Her smile increased considerably. Sitting up in

her chair, Maya rested her elbows on the desk, her gaze pinned on him. "Then you do realize that your career could be shut down? Terminated? The U.S. Army Medical Corps isn't exactly going to be pleased with your findings about us."

"I know that, ma'am."

"They'll conveniently get rid of you, Sergeant. They'll sandbag your career. You know that?"

Burke frowned. "That's one scenario that could play out. Yes, ma'am."

"Sergeant, I called you in here to give you a choice. To save your army career if that's what you want. I'm sure after they get your report, you'll be quietly removed from your post as a teacher. They'll ship you off to some part of the world where you'll not be seen or heard from again. And they'll bury your report." Maya lost her smile. "I know what I'm talking about, Sergeant. People who have vision aren't always what the army really wants."

Burke gazed into her narrowed green eyes. "Okay, what're my options, then?"

Shrugging delicately, Maya said, "I could, if you want, put in a request for your transfer—to stay here with us, Sergeant. We need a second paramedic. The squadron is growing by leaps and bounds because the U.S. Army is utilizing us as a combat training squadron now, so we have lots more people here than before. I'm looking to get a second M.D. down here, to help Dr. Cornell, as well.''

Maya sized him up and drawled, ''I like you, Gifford. You show courage in the face of fire. You aren't afraid of the truth even if it's different from what you thought or expected. Would you like to work with Sergeant Paredes? She would be your superior, of course, due to her time in grade here, but you two seem to get along very nicely anyway. Or am I wrong?''

Gulping, Burke stood there, his mind racing. Shocked by the major's unexpected offer, he murmured, ''No, ma'am, you're not wrong. In fact, to be honest, I love her. I…uh, well, I didn't know what I was going to do about it. I was going to go back to my base and ask my commanding officer for a transfer down to here, to be with her.''

''That's what I thought.''

Burke stared at her. He had heard that Maya could read minds. Now he believed it.

''Sit down, Gifford.'' Maya gestured to a chair that stood against the wall. ''And shut the door, will you?''

He knew about Maya's open-door policy—how anyone who wanted to talk to her could, whether a lowly private or an officer. Shutting the door quietly, he picked up the chair, set it near the corner of her desk and sat down. His heart was pounding in his chest. He hadn't even told Angel of his plans because he didn't want to disappoint her.

"Okay," Maya said, leaning back in her chair, "here's what I can do for you. I can pull some career strings, thanks to some friends in powerful positions, to get you down here. You're still going to have to go back to your superiors, deliver your report and go through with the paperwork. By the time you arrive back at your base, my request to have you transferred to us will be in the works. Your C.O. will know about it before you ever hand him that report."

Burke leaned forward, hands clasped between his open thighs. "That way they won't get the opportunity to sweep me quietly under the rug."

"Bingo. You got it." Maya smiled thinly. "Does Angel know you love her?"

"She knows."

"Is it mutual?"

"Yes, ma'am, it is."

"I thought so." Maya smiled slightly. "I think you need a little quality time with one another, away from this place. You need to tell her about your decision and what's going to happen. On the mining side of our mountain, we have a group of company houses. Our married personnel live over there. We reserve one house as an R and R site. Because you're paramedics, I can't authorize both of you to leave BJS at the same time, because we're on a wartime footing here and I may need you. The best I can do is give you forty-eight hours of liberty over at the R and R house. If we need you, you'll be nearby and can render Dr. Cornell the assistance she requires with anyone who gets injured.''

''That's more than fair,'' Burke murmured. In the past month, he and Angel had had few chances to be alone together. Stolen kisses every now and then was as good as it got.

''And then you'll have to go back to the States. I don't know how long your transfer will take, but I'm thinking less than a month. You need to tell Angel all this. I'm assuming you're looking down the road at asking her to marry you?''

Nodding, Burke said, ''Absolutely.''

''Okay,'' Maya said, ''whenever that happens, you'll get base housing on the mining side. You'll have your own home while stationed here with us.''

''My enlistment is up in a year, ma'am. If the U.S. Army thinks it's going to send me somewhere other than here, I won't let it happen.''

''Angel wouldn't like it, anyway. She's Peruvian

army, and they're not about to send her out of the country to be with you, even if you're married by that time.''

''I know,'' Burke said. ''I've been doing a little digging around about that.''

Maya grinned. ''You're a good man, Burke. I'll do what I can to help you and Angel. She's a wonderful person, one I think highly of. She's saved a lot of lives here at BJS over the years. I like seeing her smile, seeing her happy.''

''I love her, ma'am. And I'm going to do my best to always keep her that way.''

''Okay, Sergeant, sounds good to me. Dismissed. Your forty-eight hours of R and R at the house begins right now. I'll tell Dr. Cornell what's up, and where she can contact you two in case she needs your help. In the meantime, I'd hunt up Angel and take off for that house pronto, if I were you.''

Smiling slightly, Burke stood and came to attention. ''I will, ma'am. Thank you…for everything.''

''Get out of here, Sergeant. You've just lost five minutes with the woman you love.''

''This is our home away from home,'' Burke told Angel as he led her into the small, cozy house near the base of the mountain. The house had hardwood floors and was sparsely furnished with bamboo furniture. The drapes were a cheery pale yellow with green bamboo shoots painted on the cloth. In the living room, a white alpaca rug lay near the fireplace.

Holding Burke's hand, Angel looked around. "What's going on, Burke? Why are we here?"

Smiling, he turned and placed his arms around her, drawing her near. Angel was wearing her green T-shirt and cammies, but that didn't take away from her beauty. "Major Stevenson is giving us forty-eight hours together. Come here, let's sit down on the couch. I have a lot to tell you."

Angel settled comfortably on the gold-colored couch. She held Burke's hands as he sat facing her, his knees against hers. The look in his eyes was one of elation. Heart soaring, she cherished this private moment with him. Their times together were so few and far between.

A month after his injury, all that was left of his wound was a pink, shiny scar. Burke had full use of his arm again, to Angel's great relief.

"First of all," he told her in a low, serious tone, "I want you to know I love you, sweetheart."

She grinned. "You tell me that every day, Burke."

"I know. But I want to tell you a hundred times

a day, Angel. Not just during stolen moments now and then when people aren't around.''

Drowning in his dark gray eyes, she whispered, ''So what's different? Why are we here?''

''Maya gave us permission to stay here for the next two days,'' Burke said. Moving his fingers slowly over her smaller ones, he felt a ripple of anxiety run through him. ''In the last month, we've let ourselves love one another. I know we're both afraid, for different reasons, but we went ahead anyway.''

Nodding, Angel felt a wave of sadness move through her. ''You're telling me all of this because in forty-eight hours, you're leaving, aren't you? Maya is giving us quality time to say goodbye to one another.'' Choking back tears, she searched Burke's face. How much she had fallen in love with this man! The last month had been heaven—and hell. Angel didn't fool herself; she knew his time here was limited.

Releasing one of her hands, Burke dug into the pocket of his cammies. Producing a small, green velvet box, he said, ''Hold on. Don't jump to conclusions, Angel. Here, I've been waiting to give you this. Go ahead, open it....'' Holding his breath, he released her hands as she took the small box.

Angel gave him a confused look as she pried

open the lid. Then she gasped. "Oh, Burke!" Inside the box was a small diamond solitaire engagement ring and a simple gold wedding band. Mouth dropping open, she jerked her head up and stared at him in disbelief.

"Do you like them?" How desperately he wanted her to! Last week, he'd flown into Cuzco on a milk run with one of the pilots, and had gone to a jewelry store and bought them.

Tears jammed Angel's eyes. "But," she whispered, her voice terribly off-key, "why are you giving these to me? You're leaving soon."

Framing her face with his hands, Burke told her about Maya's offer. He watched as the tears ran down Angel's cheeks. Just the way she held the box gently in her cupped hands told him all he wanted to know.

"I'm coming back to you," he said gruffly. "Maya has given us forty-eight hours here alone with one another. I figure it might take a month to get back down here, but when I do, she's assigning us a house to live in together. I know we need more time, Angel. You don't have to marry me right away. Just know that my commitment to you is serious. Lifelong if you want."

"Oh, Burke..." Angel sobbed. Leaning forward, she placed a warm, wet kiss on his grim-looking mouth. Instantly he drew her against him, his mouth cherishing hers. Holding the rings, Angel wrapped her arms around him. "I love you so much! This is a dream come true! I never thought...well, I never thought this would have a happy ending. I— I was trying to prepare myself for your leaving."

Kissing her hair, Burke smoothed it with his hand. "I know, sweetheart. I know. So was I. But your leader is a pretty smart woman. It's like she knew about us."

Laughing, Angel eased out of his arms and smiled as she wiped the tears of happiness from her eyes. "Maya knows everything. I told you—she reads minds."

"She thinks the world of you, Angel. And I know she wants you to be happy." Caressing her damp cheek, Burke whispered, "So do I. I want to see those stars dancing in your dark brown eyes. I want to see your love for me reflected in them."

Sniffing, Angel picked up the solitaire. "Put it on my finger, Burke?"

"You sure?"

"I've never been more sure of anything in my life as I am this." She held out her left hand.

Joy surged through Burke as he gently slid the ring onto her finger. "There. It's official now."

Blinking back her tears, Angel looked at it. The

light glanced off the small, round diamond, creating a miniature rainbow of colors. "It's so beautiful, Burke. It's perfect."

"There's no rush to get married, you know. I'm going to be happy just living with you until you feel it's the right time."

She laughed a little. "Well, down here in Peru, a one-year engagement is standard procedure. We need to see my family. You need to ask my parents for my hand in marriage."

"I'll do all of that," Burke promised her seriously. "I want your family to be a part of this, Angel. They love you and so do I. I don't mind waiting a year."

Sitting back, Angel looked at the engagement ring on her hand. "I never thought, Burke, that I'd love again. Not after…well, what happened."

He placed the ring box on the glass coffee table in front of the couch. Picking up her hands, Burke saw that her brows were drawn with pain. "You had a broken heart, Angel. So did I. We were both deeply wounded by people and by circumstances." Pressing a warm kiss to her fingers, he lifted his head and whispered, "But you know what? We had the courage to reach out to one another and try again. That's what's important."

"Living life is not for the weak," she agreed

quietly, studying the long, strong hands enclos-
ing hers.

"And I'm looking forward to a long and very
exciting life with you." Burke got up and walked
into the other room. When he came back, he handed
Angel a two-pound box of chocolates.

"Oh!" Angel whispered, holding the box, in
shock. "My favorite! Truffles!"

She gazed wonderingly up at him. Burke had a
cockeyed smile on his mouth.

"Yeah, Snake told me where I could buy you a
box when I was in Cuzco to get the rings."

Running her fingers reverently across the box,
Angel whispered, "You remembered..."

Burke moved toward her, his voice low. "I always want to remember the things that bring that
smile to your face, sweetheart."

His words thrilled Angel, suffusing her heart with
a hope she never thought she'd feel. Lifting her
head, she drowned in his warm gray gaze. "I want
to love you, Burke. Let's go to the bedroom?"

Grinning, he released her hands and stood up.
"Come here, woman." And he swept her up in his
arms. Angel gave a gasp of surprise and quickly
grabbed his shoulders. She was small compared to
him, a lightweight. Feeling her rounded, firm body
against his, her head resting against his neck and

shoulder, Burke smiled as he walked through the house. His boots thunked hollowly on the polished wooden floor as he moved past the kitchen and bathroom to the large bedroom beyond. Entering it, he stood in the doorway.

"Well, what do you think?" And he smiled down at her.

Angel looked around. In the center of the room was a large queen-size bed with mahogany headboard and footer, a cream-colored alpaca blanket spread across it. The drapes were a light lavender, the creamy wallpaper sprinkled with tiny violets. "I like it."

"So do I." Burke sat her down on the bed.

Angel spotted a large, glass-enclosed shower in the adjacent bathroom. "You know what?" she said wickedly as she began to unlace her boots. "I'd love to make love with you in that nice, hot shower. How about it?"

Grinning, Burke got rid of his own boots and set them off to one side. "Sounds like a plan to me...." Turning, he helped ease the green T-shirt over Angel's head. She wore a simple white cotton camisole beneath it, and no bra. The look in her eyes was one of need—for him. She stood up and unbuttoned her cammies with trembling fingers. He did the same.

Their clothes fell in separate piles as they undressed. When Angel had pulled off her camisole and dropped it, she reached over and gripped Burke's large hand.

"Come on. Let's take a shower together...."

Liking her boldness and earthiness, Burke led her into the white-tiled bathroom. Opening the shower door, he turned on the faucets. In no time, steam was permeating the large enclosure. Stepping in, he pulled Angel along with him and then closed the glass door. Streams of warm water pummeled them like soft pelting raindrops as he turned and drew her into his arms.

"You are so beautiful to me," Burke whispered, closing his mouth over hers. Just feeling Angel step into his arms, her mouth boldly meeting his, her body fusing against his larger, harder one, sent a river of scalding heat rippling wildly through Burke.

The moment her breasts glided against his massive, hairy chest, a shiver went through Angel, and she nearly drowned in the heat and wetness of his kiss. The water fell gently across them, making her hands slick as she ran them up his shoulders and around his neck to tangle in his short, dark hair. His mouth hungrily plundered hers. And when his male hardness pressed against her abdomen, proving his desire for her, she was lost. A pounding urgency coiled hotly within her.

The steam, the heat, the wetness of the shower combined with the scalding need that grew within Angel as he worshipped her mouth. When his large, callused hands ranged upward from her hips and waist to caress her breasts, she gasped.

"You taste so good to me," Burke rasped thickly against her lips. Lifting Angel away from him, he leaned down and captured the taut peak of one of her small, firm breasts with his mouth. He heard her give a cry of pleasure. Her hands gripped his shoulders hard, her fingers digging frantically into his tense flesh. Suckling her, feeling her become warm and pliable in his grasp, Burke absorbed her cries and her wild, unfettered response.

"I need you, Burke!" Angel gasped, opening her eyes. His own eyes were slits, silvered and stormy-looking. She slid her arms tighter around his neck. "I want you... Take me now—please...." And she moved sinuously against his taut body, feeling him tense, hearing him groan her name. Then his hands settled firmly around her waist and in one smooth, unbroken motion, he lifted her up against him. Wrapping her legs around his narrow hips, Angel pressed her mouth to his, her tongue moving boldly, causing his massive control to snap.

The moment he slid into her sleek, moist confines, Angel threw back her head, her lips parting as white-hot pleasure rippled through her. Oh, the joy of mating with Burke! He held her gently for precious seconds, allowing her body to accommodate him. Gasping, Angel closed her eyes, the warm streams of water cascading against her face and soaking into her hair.

Moments later she felt his power as he entered her completely. Sliding slowly against him, up and down, with his strong, caring hands cupping her hips and guiding her, made Angel spin into a universe where only joy, heat and pleasure existed. Closing her eyes, her cheek against his, she moaned with every slow, delicious movement he choreographed. The sun and moon collided within her; she felt the warmth of the water trickling down around them, embracing them. And when Burke groaned, the sound reverberated like a drum through her singing body. Clinging to him, enjoying the chaotic pleasure throbbing through her, Angel surrendered to him fully.

The moment she did, she felt a surprising flare of scalding heat erupt deep within her. Burke felt it, too, for he groaned again and crushed her against him. The air collapsed from her lungs as she clung to him, her face pressed against his jaw. The world spun wildly behind her closed eyes as she felt a tumult of white-hot heat thrum through her in throbbing tidal waves of light and joy. Burke gripped her hard, the warmth of the water spilling around them like a stroking hand.

Long moments fused together as they clung silently to one another in the aftermath. Angel felt Burke gently ease her away from him. As her feet touched the shower floor, she leaned heavily against him, unsure if she could stand. Head resting on his chest, she heard the solid pounding of his heart. Wrapping her arms around him, she was content to enjoy the feel of the water, of his warm, solid body and his cradling arms. She felt an intense inner glow, as if the sun itself were burning brightly within her. Angel smiled, more than satisfied.

Burke leaned down and pressed several kisses against her wet hair and cheek. "I love you, Angel. You're mine. I'm yours."

Nodding, she couldn't find her voice. All she could do was run her hands up and down Burke's arms. Time ceased to exist as she rested languidly against his body, absorbing every nuance of him.

Eventually, Burke found the soap and began to slather it across Angel's neck, shoulders and arms. When she stepped back, he saw that her dark eyes were velvety with love—for him. Moving his hands slowly up and down her strong, slim arms, he discovered that washing her was a delightful new experience for him. As he lathered soap across her back, torso and breasts, he heard her sigh. Yes, this was like making love to her all over again, and Burke thought it was a delicious way to prolong the feelings he held for her.

Later, as they stepped from the shower after washing one another thoroughly, Burke took a pale yellow bath towel and wrapped Angel snugly within its soft, thick folds. Lifting her into his arms, he carried her out of the bathroom and deposited her gently on the bed. Her hair was damp and he took his towel and began to gently dry it.

Reaching up, Angel ran her hands across his glistening shoulders, wiping away the beads of water. "I like making love with you," she sighed.

"Me, too." Burke grinned crookedly as he patted drops of water from her brow and cheeks. "We need to do this often."

"Oh, yes," Angel whispered. "I like being washed by you."

"You're kinda good at it, too."

"Yeah?"

"Oh, yeah…"

"Lie down with me? Just hold me, Burke?"

How easy it was to tuck her within the fluffy

yellow towel and then bring her fully against him. "There. Is that better?" Burke rested against the pillow after positioning Angel's head in the crook of his shoulder.

"Mmm, much…" she said, closing her eyes and sliding her arm around his damp torso.

As Burke lay there with Angel in his arms, he closed his eyes and savored the strength of her small, beautiful body so close to his own. Pressing a kiss against her damp hair, he leaned over and whispered, "I'm going to love you forever, Angel. A crazy kind of fate brought us together, and I'm glad we had the guts to open up to one another and try to love again."

Opening her eyes, Angel absorbed the love burning in his eyes—love for her alone. She caressed his cheek, feeling the sandpapery texture beneath her fingers. "I am, too, darling. You hold my heart in your hands. I need nothing else in life but that…and you."

Epilogue

"Angel, you're going TDY—temporary duty—while Sergeant Gifford is up north in the U.S.A."

"Ma'am?" Standing at ease in front of her C.O.'s desk, Angel stared wide-eyed in surprise. Yesterday, Burke had left to deliver his fact-finding report to his superiors. Her heart had nearly broken, she'd miss him so much. Angel had to continually remind herself that he'd be returning a month from now—for good.

Smiling as she rummaged through the stacks of paper on her desk, Maya said, "I'm sending you for some extracurricular training, Sergeant. You've heard of the Village of the Clouds? The Jaguar Clan training center?''

''Well sure...'' Angel's mind spun with the news. With surprise and delight. She saw a grin hover on Maya's lips as she dropped a bunch of papers into the Out basket on her desk.

''You're familiar with the village, I assume?''

''Sort of...'' Angel began, excitement threading through her. ''My mother went when she was very young, for a couple of years, to train with mystical teachers who live there.''

''That's right, she's a jaguar priestess,'' Maya murmured, sitting back, the chair creaking and protesting loudly. ''And so are you.'' Her eyes narrowed speculatively on Angel. ''You just took a different route to receive the training, that's all. When your jaguar guide showed up while you were on the run from the drug soldiers, and you were able to stop Burke from bleeding out, I figured it was time.''

''Time?''

''Yeah. For you to get your butt up there and begin more formalized training to develop your skills fully. I figure you'll be pining away for Sergeant Gifford for a whole month, so I'm gonna take advantage of this lull in your relationship and send you there. It will keep you not only entertained, but focused and busy as hell. You won't have much free time to miss your man. At the end of thirty days, you'll be back here to meet him as he arrives at the Cuzco airport. Fair enough?''

Angel was at a loss for words. "Well, er, sure, Major...that's wonderful. I mean...dude, this is so cool...."

Maya grinned. "I didn't think you'd mind."

"But," Angel said worriedly, "what about BJS? You need a paramedic. We can't both be gone at the same time."

Holding up her hand, Maya said, "Relax, I've got all the bases covered on that one. We have an emergency-room physician, Captain Neal Gates from the U.S. Army, comin' in to train with Dr. Cornell for the next month."

"Great!" Angel exclaimed. She grinned and rubbed her hands together. "Thank you, Major. I won't let this opportunity go to waste."

"Better not," Maya growled good-naturedly, "because your parents are expecting great things of you, too." She raised her black brows. "It'll just make your Angel of Death legend even *more* impressive than it has already become."

Just then the executive officer for BJS, Lieutenant Dallas Klein, peeked into the office, a dark look on her face. "Er...I'd better go, Major," Angel said. "Looks like you're pretty busy around here right now."

Maya gestured for Dallas to enter. "Yeah, I am, Angel. Meet me down at the takeoff lip in thirty minutes. We'll fly to Agua Caliente, where the gateway to the Village of the Clouds is located."

"Yes, ma'am!" Angel came to attention, saluted and did an about-face. She nodded in Dallas's direction and practically floated out of the office.

"You're lookin' damned unhappy," Maya noted sourly of her X.O.

"I'm shutting your door. I just got some disturbing news."

"Oh…more. I can hardly wait. Seems to be the day for it. Sit down…."

"I'm on the run, Maya. This'll take just a second."

"Okay, shoot."

Dallas sat on the edge of Maya's desk, scowling. "You had wanted me to contact Morgan Trayhern about that black ops mission we're putting together up in central Mexico."

"Right," Maya said, picking up her cup and sipping the now lukewarm coffee.

"Things are fine along mission lines," Dallas assured her. She moved her fingers distractedly through her dark brown, slightly curly hair. "But

Morgan sounded really upset when I talked to him. Over the last year, he's been more like a friend to me than, well, you know..."

"Yeah, Morgan has a way of making friends with many people he works with," Maya agreed. "So why is he so upset?"

"I finally got up the guts to ask him about it." Shrugging, Dallas said, "I don't normally nose around in his personal business...."

"Ha! As an X.O., that's *all* you do—sniff out trouble, discontent and all that stuff."

Chuckling, Dallas said, "Guilty as charged. Well, I asked. And here's what Morgan told me. We're to hold it in confidence."

"Not a problem. Personal stuff?"

"Yeah," Dallas sighed. "You know his oldest son, Jason Trayhern?"

"Sure. He's at the Naval Academy. Third year, I think."

"He isn't anymore...."

"What?" Maya sat up straight. Scowling, she growled, "What happened?"

"Jason was named as one of the cadets caught smuggling that rave drug to his classmates."

Maya came out of her chair. "No way! Jason wouldn't do that!"

"That's what Morgan said. His son is a straight

arrow when it comes to drugs. He's never touched them.''

"Wait a minute," Maya said. "Was he framed?''

"Morgan doesn't know for sure. The upshot of it is that Jason was fingered, and when he went before the review board at the academy, he refused to name the people who were dealing the drug.''

"But…that doesn't mean *he* was dealing! Maybe it was a roommate or somethin'?''

"Sounds like it," Dallas said sadly. Opening her hands, she said, "But because Jason refused to indict the guilty parties, he was booted out of the academy along with the rest of the accused young men.''

"Oh, God…" Maya muttered, sitting back down. "Morgan *has* to be crushed. I mean, every firstborn son in his family has gone to one of the academies since they've been built in America. What a blow for him and his family.''

"I've never heard him sound so upset," Dallas said sympathetically. "He had such high hopes for Jason to carry on the family name and all.''

Rubbing her chin, Maya stared at Dallas. "Jason is like most academy students. They have this stupid idea that ratting on your fellow students is breaking the code of honor. He's wrong. It's a flawed system and the code's screwed up about when to invoke this rule and when not to.''

"Yeah, in my book a code of honor doesn't cover misdeeds. Sounds as if he can't sort out bad from good. What's the point of a code if it doesn't protect the good guys? Jason should have come clean if he knew who was doing this.''

"No argument from me. I have to call Morgan. He's going to need some support.''

"The man talked to me for twenty minutes,'' Dallas said. "And I'm sure he can use as many sympathetic ears as he can get.''

Shaking her head, Maya muttered, "God, they just got past surviving that earthquake out in Southern California, where Laura was trapped and almost died. That poor family seems to swing from one emotional cliff-hanger to another.''

"I think,'' Dallas said with a slight smile, "that perhaps Laura might need a sympathetic ear right now as well. You might call her, too. She thinks so much of you, and I know she could probably use a lot of support herself right now.''

"Good idea,'' Maya said, looking at the phone on her desk. "I'll call Laura first, find out the lay of the land. Then I'll call Morgan, tomorrow maybe.''

Nodding, Dallas eased off the desk, smoothing

the fabric of her black, one-piece flight suit. "I feel so badly for the whole family."

"What about Jason? Is he home now?"

Shaking her head, Dallas said, "No. He's refusing to go home. Apparently there's a lot of friction between him and Morgan. They had a huge fight."

"I feel sorry for him, too," Maya said. "This can't be easy on him. What's he going to do, do you know?"

Shrugging, Dallas said, "I think Morgan said Jason was going to enlist in the army warrant officer program and try to qualify to fly Apache helicopters."

Brightening, Maya said, "Good choice. I remember he said he always loved to fly, so maybe this is best for him. We can always use a damn good Apache pilot." She grinned wryly. "Who knows? Jason might end up down here with us for advance combat training. Wouldn't that be a hoot?"

Shaking her head, Dallas opened the office door, then hesitated. "I think Jason is hurrying from one bad gig to another and not giving himself the time he needs to work through this whole mess. Running off to the army is okay, but my sense is he needs some downtime to sort out his priorities and what he really wants out of life—not what his dad wants him to be. My sense is he's still rebelling against

Morgan by going into the army as something less than an officer. Warrants are way down in rank. That's a slap in the face to Morgan, given the family expectations.''

Nodding, Maya said, ''Yeah, I know Morgan puts a lot of demands on him. And Jason wouldn't be the first young person to run off to a military service to escape going home.''

''Granted,'' Dallas said. She waved to Maya. ''I've got a lot of things up in the air. I'll leave you to make your phone call. Just keep me in the loop, okay? The Trayherns are good people. I hate to see bad things happening to them. They don't deserve it.''

Snorting, Maya said, ''Who does? I've always said bad things happen to good people.''

''True, and life ain't fair.'' Dallas waved shortly. ''Adios…''

''Yeah. Later, amiga…''

Maya stared at the black phone. This was shocking and tragic news. How many times had Morgan proudly bragged to her of Jason's accomplishments at the academy during their many phone calls? He doted on his oldest son. Maybe Morgan hadn't communicated his fatherly pride to Jason.

Sighing, Maya placed her hand on the phone. Laura would be devastated for other reasons, she surmised. Right now, Laura had a new, adopted infant in the household, and she was still recovering from her injuries in the earthquake. Now this… The black mark of Jason being kicked out of a prestigious military academy was going to follow him around like a cloud for the rest of his life. It would be a terrible burden to carry. And running off to join the army air corps wasn't going to make it any easier. Maya was sure that the army would snatch Jason up, because he was a third-year academy student; he had the right stuff. But they'd be watching him, too. If he made any trouble, they wouldn't tolerate it and they'd boot him out. At the same time, Maya knew that the army would give Jason a chance to prove he wasn't into drugs, wasn't a rebel without a cause. She wished only the best for him. Right now, the Trayherns were a family of broken hearts, and she ached for all of them.

Picking up the phone, Maya dialed the number that would put her in touch with Laura. While she waited for the call to go through, her mind swung back to the Angel of Death. A slight smile pulled at her mouth. Angel and Burke had a wonderful life laid out before them. Thirty days apart would only strengthen their love for one another.

And best of all, Maya would have them here, at BJS, with her. They were fine people and she wanted them happy. Maya knew there were dark periods and light ones in everyone's life. Angel and Burke had each gone through their own dark night of the soul. And when they'd found one another, they'd had the courage to reach out and allow themselves to love once more.

Life was never fair, but Maya knew the gift of love made it all worthwhile. People only needed the courage to reach for love and not be afraid of it. And she hoped Jason Trayhern had the same kind of internal fortitude and courage. Maya turned from the unhappy events, her mind lingering over the coming month when Burke and Angel would be united. They were going to make a strong, indelible impression down here for BJS and she was glad that it worked out for them. Angel had always carried a deep sadness in her and now it was gone. Smiling a little, Maya picked up a report and set it in front of her. Burke would love Angel forever and a day after that…no question.…

* * * * *

Coming in March 2003 from
USA TODAY *bestselling author*
LINDSAY McKENNA

A brand-new book in the
MORGAN'S MERCENARIES:
DESTINY'S WOMEN
saga!

AN HONORABLE WOMAN

Turn the page for a sneak preview...

Chapter 1

Cam turned to Chief Warrant Officer Gus Morales. Her heart sped up, but it wasn't out of fear. It was something else, some other feeling that emerged so quickly under the pressured circumstances, that Cam couldn't name it. As she looked into his warm cinnamon-colored eyes and saw the slightest hint of a smile on his full, well-shaped mouth, she struggled to keep her voice low and firm.

"Chief Morales?" she asked. "Can you tell me about your flight experience?"

"Ma'am, I was born in a helicopter."

She looked at him and blinked once. "Excuse me?"

Gus grinned and opened his hands. "My mother

is Yaqui Indian, from northern Mexico. She was visiting her family in the desolate area where they lived when she went into labor with me. My father, who is a U.S. Army helicopter pilot, flew her out when her water broke. He was hoping to fly to Nogales, and then across the border into Texas to get her to the hospital on time.''

Cam smiled a little. ''Don't tell me? You were actually born in the helo?''

He liked her smile. There wasn't anything not to like about her, Gus decided. That pale sprinkling of freckles across her broad cheekbones, the way her hair glinted with red and gold highlights even beneath the washed-out fluorescent light above them. Chief Morales suddenly looked a lot less threatening than she had earlier.

''Yes, ma'am. By the time my father landed the helo on the top of the hospital's roof, she'd given birth to me.'' Gus's smile widened. ''The attendants who came out were kinda surprised.''

''That's a great story, Chief Morales. So, did the helicopter ride stay in your blood?'' Cam liked the way his eyes crinkled, and his dimples showed as he smiled fully.

''Yes, ma'am, it did. My father flew civilian helicopters for the civil Air Patrol in his free time. I got my helo license when I was thirteen years old, when my legs were long enough to reach the pedals.''

''I see,'' Cam said, trying not to sound impressed. But she was. The natural warmth and openness of Morales compared to the other two pilots was like night and day. Cam realized instantly that he didn't have a problem with her being a woman and his C.O. like the other two did.

But she realized *she* might have a problem with her attraction to Chief Morales....

* * * * *

USA TODAY bestselling author

LINDSAY McKENNA

**brings you a brand-new series
featuring Morgan Trayhern and his team!**

WOMAN OF INNOCENCE
(Silhouette Special Edition #1442)

An innocent beauty longing for adventure. A rugged mercenary
sworn to protect her. A romantic adventure like no other!

DESTINY'S WOMAN
(Silhouette Books)

A Native American woman with a wounded heart. A strong, loving
soldier with a sheltering embrace. A love powerful enough to heal…

Available in Feburary!

HER HEALING TOUCH
(Silhouette Special Edition #1519)

A legendary healer. A Special Forces paramedic in need of faith
in love. A passion so strong it could not be denied…

Available in March!

AN HONORABLE WOMAN
(Silhouette Books)

A beautiful pilot with a plan to win back her honor. The man who
stands by her side through and through. The mission that would
take them places no heart should dare go alone…

Silhouette®
Where love comes alive™

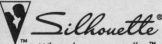

If you enjoyed what you just read,
then we've got an offer you can't resist!

Take 2 bestselling love stories FREE!

Plus get a FREE surprise gift!

SPECIAL EDITION